"*Let me prove it to you!*"

"With a kiss?" Emma struggled angrily in Patrick's arms. "Go to hell! I know precisely what a kiss from you will lead to!"

"Yes, so do I!" Patrick pulled her hard against him. "That's precisely why I'm going to do it. To force you to acknowledge just how strong the bond between us really is!"

Emma stopped struggling. "What bond? There is no bond...."

"There is, and you know it!"

SARAH HOLLAND was born in Kent, southern England, and brought up in London. She began writing at eighteen because she loved the warmth and excitement of Harlequin Mills & Boon. She has traveled the world, living in Hong Kong, the south of France and Holland. She attended drama school, and was a nightclub singer and a songwriter. She now lives on the Isle of Man. Her hobbies are acting, singing, painting and psychology. She loves noisy dinner parties, buying clothes and being busy.

SARAH HOLLAND

Master of Seduction

Harlequin Books

TORONTO • NEW YORK • LONDON
AMSTERDAM • PARIS • SYDNEY • HAMBURG
STOCKHOLM • ATHENS • TOKYO • MILAN
MADRID • WARSAW • BUDAPEST • AUCKLAND

FOR
Karen Patricia White

ISBN 0-373-18651-7

MASTER OF SEDUCTION

First North American Publication 1997.

Copyright © 1995 by Sarah Holland.

This edition published by arrangement with Harlequin Books S.A.

® and TM are trademarks of the publisher. Trademarks indicated with ® are registered in the United States Patent and Trademark Office, the Canadian Trade Marks Office and in other countries.

Printed in U.S.A.

CHAPTER ONE

THE white Citroën taxi drew up on the *quai* of St Tropez. A row of glittering white yachts bobbed gently in the warm harbour waters, while opposite them sat hundreds of people at the jaunty cafés lining the street, sipping Perrier and watching the rich go by.

Emma stepped out of the car, scarlet sundress fluttering in the hot breeze, drawing attention to her long, slim legs. Her hair was black as night, long and curvy, framing a beautiful, classical face with cat-green eyes and a full, firm mouth.

'I'll pay the fare,' Liz said with a bright smile. 'You go to the yacht and ask for some help with the cases.'

Emma stared blankly at the row of luxury yachts. 'Which one is it?'

'Oh—sorry. The big one in the middle. It's called *Sea Witch*.'

Turning, Emma walked quickly along the hot stone *quai*, looking up at the yachts with a bemused smile.

All this reminded her of her childhood, when her rich father would pamper and parade her to all his rich friends, and she would play the beloved daughter for his benefit. The only trouble was, she had been very far from beloved. She had been more of a pretty little doll for him to dress in expensive clothes, and the artifice of that world was akin to the glittering artifice of these magnificent yachts. It was an artifice she had rejected when her father died, and one she did not wish to return to.

It therefore seemed ironic to walk along the *quai* looking for the yacht she would be cruising on for the next two weeks with Liz's elder brother, Patrick.

Liz was her best friend and also, currently, her employer. Liz wrote romantic novels. Emma detested them. But she also detested an unproductive life, and when her previous job as a secretary had come to a conclusion in January Liz's secretary had resigned. It had seemed the perfect solution for Emma to begin working for Liz.

She had been working for Liz for six months now, and, while she found the general soppiness of romantic novels absurd, she loved spending every day with her friend.

When Liz's elder brother had telephoned from America last week to invite Liz on this cruise, Liz had invited Emma. Emma had been delighted to accept, thinking the yacht would be a small and unpretentious craft.

But now she felt swamped by waves of nasty *déjà vu* as she strolled along the quayside looking for the glittering white multi-million dollar palace of a yacht called *Sea Witch*.

Suddenly, she was in front of it.

Two people, a man and a woman, sat on white chairs on the deck drinking cocktails. The man was bare-chested with dark hair, and the woman was a glamorous brunette with red lips. They both wore sunglasses.

Emma cleared her throat. 'Excuse me—I'm Emma Baccarat, Liz Kinsella's secretary, and——'

'About bloody time,' drawled the brunette. 'We've been waiting around all day. It's gone four and we were supposed to sail at three!'

Emma steeled herself to be polite. 'Perhaps you should take that up with the airline. It was hardly my fault the flight was delayed. In the meantime, we need some help with our cases. Could anyone lend us a hand?'

'Yes, I'll come and help.' The man got to his feet, revealing himself to be an astonishingly handsome giant, at least six feet six, as he strode, rippling with solid muscle, down the wooden gangplank.

Emma stared at him from behind her dark glasses.

He was the best-looking man she had ever seen. A living archetype of powerful masculinity, with that body, that tough face and that height. Suntan oil sheened his bare, bronzed chest, gleaming on black hairs and solid muscle, down to the flat brown stomach above his faded jeans.

He stopped in front of her, towering over her with a cool, condescending smile. 'I'm Patrick Kinsella.'

This arrogant giant was Liz's brother? Emma just stared at him, stupefied, and racked her brains to try to remember everything she had ever heard or read about him.

Meanwhile, Patrick smiled cynically, obviously taking her silence for swooning over his extraordinary looks. 'Patrick Kinsella,' he drawled again, clearly pleased by the sound of his own name, and extended a huge hand, adding, 'Delighted to meet you—welcome aboard.'

'Thank you.' Emma shook his hand irritably, deciding he was not only loathsome, but devoid of any moral values, if he was involved with that appalling woman who had just been so rude to her. 'It was kind of you to invite me on your yacht, Mr Kinsella.'

'Call me Patrick.'

'Patrick.' She smiled coldly as she dropped his vast hand. His name was about all he had going for him, as far as she was concerned. Emma's mother had been Irish, and Emma had long felt a deep connection with Ireland, something that would have bordered on romanticism, if she had ever felt the slightest bit romantic. Still, at least his accent wasn't Irish—it was pure upper-class English, and therefore had not the slightest effect on her.

With a cold, polite smile she said, 'I'm very much looking forward to the cruise. I understand we'll be stopping in Morocco?'

'Among other places.' He gave a cool nod, then lifted his dark head. 'Is that my sister over there with ten million suitcases?'

'Yes.' Emma turned to look at Liz perched like a pixie on a pile of suitcases, her short dark bobbed hair flickering around her gamine face, waving cheerfully at her brother.

They walked over to her together; or rather Emma swayed and Patrick strode like some unidentified species of jungle cat, his powerful body so packed with hard muscle that Emma regarded him through her dark glasses with the same cool detachment with which one might study an animal in a zoo.

'Hi, Liz!' Bending a long, long distance, Patrick dropped a kiss on his sister's cheek. 'You're looking very well. Must be all that romantic nonsense you spend your time dreaming about.'

'Don't be horrid.' Liz leapt up from the cases, laughing. 'Anyway, you wait. One day you'll fall in love when you're least expecting it, and then you won't be quite so pleased with yourself. Have you met Emma?'

'Yes, we just introduced ourselves,' Patrick said, without glancing at Emma. 'I've postponed sailing till midnight tonight because I wasn't sure what time you'd get here. Meanwhile, Charles and Toby have gone up to the old fort for the afternoon. Natasha's the only one on board.'

Liz made a face. 'Lord save us all from Natasha! Is she being vile, or just mildly unspeakable?'

'Mildly unspeakable,' Patrick said, then looked down at her cases. 'Is this the lot? If I take four can you two manage the rest?'

They agreed that they could, and Patrick picked up four cases in huge hands, striding away easily with them. Liz and Emma followed at a leisurely pace.

It was quite a relief to Emma to realise that the appalling brunette called Natasha was renowned for vile behaviour. She wondered why Patrick Kinsella was going out with her if he disliked her so much, and decided he was probably the kind of man who liked love-hate relationships with bitchy women. Good luck to him, she thought with an indifferent shrug.

At twenty-six years old, Emma was rather jaded in terms of love relationships. She didn't believe in romance, nor did she believe in ever finding true love.

Oh, she had a secret ideal man, but she kept him to herself, not telling anyone because she was sure he did not exist and that she would never meet him. She had no idea what he would look like: she wasn't interested in looks, she was only interested in the mind.

But most men were only interested in sex and showpiece women they could boast about to their friends. She hated artifice—she had, after all, spent most of her early life playing roles, first for her father, then for her late husband. No more role-playing for Emma—she wanted honesty or nothing.

They approached the yacht and walked up the gangplank, watched with interest by the people at the cafés, and as they reached the deck three men in white uniform suddenly appeared.

'Take these cases down to my sister's cabin.' Patrick deposited them on the deck. 'And the rest to Miss Baccarat's.'

The men nodded silently, no doubt used to being serfs for Mr Kinsella the incredible hulk, and disappeared with the cases down the long polished wood deck to a slim white door on the right-hand side.

'Would either of you like to go down to your cabins to freshen up or settle in?' Patrick studied them both from behind dark glasses.

'I'd like a drink first,' Liz told her brother. 'That journey was hell on two legs, and I see a nice magnum of champagne over there with my name on it!'

Patrick laughed, strolled coolly to the bottle, took two glasses and handed one to Liz, one to Emma. 'By the way,' he said, 'this is Natasha de Courcey. Natasha—this is Emma Baccarat.'

'Ah, yes, Miss Baccarat,' drawled Natasha. 'I suppose I ought to shake hands and say how do you do, but I frankly can't be bothered.'

'That's quite all right, Natasha.' Patrick poured champagne into Emma's glass. 'We're all used to your bad manners. Emma may as well get used to them too.'

Natasha sipped her drink, tapping one foot. 'I'm just bad-tempered because we're stuck in St Tropez for hours on end. The only thing to do here is shop, and one gets so bored spending one's husband's money.'

'One wouldn't know,' Liz drawled. 'One doesn't have a husband. Put a little more champagne in my glass, Patrick...'

'Well, we all know about your famous single status, Liz, going around dreaming of romance but never finding it. But are you married, Miss Baccarat?' Natasha arched one silver brow at Emma.

'No,' Emma said coolly, 'I'm a widow.'

'A widow!' Natasha smiled slowly, red lips curving like a nasty little pussycat's. 'Oh, how very unusual for a girl of your age! How long have you been widowed?'

'Five years.' Emma sipped her champagne, face tranquil.

Natasha de Courcey pushed her dark glasses up to reveal a pair of heavy-lidded dark eyes with malice in their depths. 'How did he die?'

'A boating accident.'

'How tragic!' Natasha said with horrible insincerity. 'What was he like?'

Emma's face was expressionless. 'He was good-looking, adventurous and he loved danger. That's why he died so young.'

'I adore men like that. Men who are mad, bad and dangerous to know. Men like Patrick...!'

Patrick gave a hard, dangerous, cynical smile, strolled to the drinks table, put the bottle of champagne down, and watched them all from behind his dark glasses in sexually menacing silence.

'Well, Miss Baccarat.' Natasha turned back to her with a nasty smile. 'Do you think you'll enjoy this cruise? I mean, you realise there's a single young man of your age on board? My brother-in-law, Toby.'

'Your brother-in-law?' Emma's brows rose and she looked at Liz. 'I thought you only had one brother?'

'I do,' Liz said, frowning, then realised what Emma had been thinking and started to laugh. 'Oh, God, what a hoot! You thought Natasha was married to Patrick? I don't believe it!'

Emma shrugged. 'Well, I naturally assumed——'

'That we were together?' Natasha laughed. 'Chance would be a fine thing! No, I'm married to Patrick and Liz's cousin Charles. His little brother is Toby, and I'm sure this is all very fated, Miss Baccarat. After all, he's single, so are you, and you're both stuck together for a fortnight on this yacht...'

Liz laughed, sipping champagne. 'I shouldn't hold out any hope for a shipboard romance between Emma and anyone. She's completely cynical, I'm afraid, and doesn't believe in love.'

'Doesn't believe in love!' Natasha was shocked. 'But how can you possibly justify that, Miss Baccarat, when you're working for a romantic novelist?'

'I initially became Liz's secretary to lend a helping hand,' Emma said, practised now in the art of explaining the conflict between her personal beliefs and her work. 'It was just going to be a temporary thing, but we work so well together that it's kind of dragged on longer than we expected.'

'Dragged on!' Liz's laughter was as bubbly as the champagne. 'You see how much she hates romance?'

'I don't hate romance,' Emma amended quickly. 'And you know I love working for you. I just don't believe in the books you write, that's all, Liz. You know what a cynic I am.'

Out of the corner of her eye, she suddenly noticed Patrick studying her with a smile on his tough mouth. Prickling, she gave him a cold, haughty look. He was the kind of man she could read like a book, and she knew precisely what that cynical smile of his meant. He thought all cynical women were available for sex without strings attached. Playboys always thought like that. Well, he could just go and playboy himself to death, if he thought *she* was that kind of woman.

Emma might have been cynical, but that didn't mean she was cheap. Far from it. She wanted truth, honesty, integrity. Real emotions, real thoughts, no pretence, no lies . . .

What was wrong with romantic love was that it wasn't the *truth*—any more than money, social position and material success were the truth. There was only one truth worth bothering with in life, and that was the fact that everyone was going to die.

Emma's eyes glided contemptuously over the handsome playboy, Patrick Kinsella, glided on past him, flickered out to the sea and sky, which were hers as long as she was alive, and far more precious than all the material success or romantic delusion in the world.

The spirit, she thought with a slow, philosophical smile, is something which cannot be bought, and which lives on after death, like a soft sea breeze on that halcyon sky. Now that's the only romance I'm prepared to believe in.

'You're not interested in romance at all?' Natasha seemed to read her mind. 'Or gorgeous, sexy men?'

Emma laughed cynically. 'Gorgeous, sexy men are always a pleasure to look at, but usually inside they're weak, selfish, vain, conceited and arrogant.' Her smile flashed contempt at Patrick Kinsella. 'I'm not interested in packaging. Only in what's inside.'

'Worthy sentiments,' drawled Natasha, 'but isn't your life a little dull without romance?'

'Hardly! I have a wonderful job, a lot of friends, opportunities for travel, and a very interesting future. What more could I ask for?'

'A man.' Natasha toyed with her glass in one red-taloned hand.

Emma smiled at her expression. Women like this little man-eater always tried to throw darts at Emma's confidence in herself, presumably because it rattled them to think that a woman could be quite happy without being obsessed by men, flirtation, romance.

'Every woman needs a man.'

'Needs?' Emma said. 'I need to eat, I need to breathe, I need to sleep—but *need* a man? No, I don't think that's a statement I can agree with. After all, I'm going to die one day, and I can't take him with me any more than I can take money or possessions or achievements.'

'All right, then!' Natasha's eyes narrowed. 'You'd *like* a man! Someone to love, to kiss, to flirt with.'

'Well, that's definitely debatable.' Emma arched cool dark brows with amusement. 'If I don't want to kiss someone, I won't, and there's an end to it.'

'And if you do want to kiss someone?' Patrick Kinsella suddenly stepped forward, pushed his dark glasses up on to his head, and she saw his eyes. She was so struck by them that she just stared at him in silence for a split-second.

Those eyes were blue—dazzling blue, steely blue, Van Gogh sky-blue, and they seemed to fill the whole deck of the yacht, the whole town of St Tropez. She could no longer see his face or the colour of his hair or even his height or bare chest.

All she could see were those eyes, blazing at her like the brightest lights she had ever seen.

They were so at odds with her initial opinion of him— a handsome, cynical, sex-obsessed playboy—that for a second she was too knocked off balance to speak.

'Cat got your tongue, Miss Baccarat?' Patrick drawled.

She quickly pulled her shattered wits together. 'If I wanted to kiss someone, I would do just that—kiss them!'

He laughed. 'Are you telling me you've never wanted to? How old are you? Twelve?'

'Well, of course I've wanted to!' she snapped, flushing hotly. 'But only when I was younger, more naïve, and believed in romance the way every teenager does.'

He was unfazed by her anger. 'Which do you hate most? Romance or sexual attraction?'

'What an impertinent question!'

'Why is it impertinent?'

'I would have thought that was perfectly obvious!'

'Because I mentioned sex? Very interesting. I think you've answered my question.'

Her face flamed. 'That's just the kind of stupid, sexist remark I'd expect from an arrogant playboy!'

'Resorting to personal insults already?' He laughed softly. 'Well, well, well. So it *is* sex that bothers you.'

'Don't you try to Freudian-analyse me, Mr Kinsella!' Her green eyes flared with temper as she pushed her dark glasses up on to her head, glaring at him. 'The truth is that I don't hate either romance *or* sexual attraction! I just see through them.'

'How do you do that?'

'What do you mean—how do I do that?' She was livid because her anger hadn't stopped him pushing at her. 'It must be perfectly obvious!'

'Not to me.'

'Then you must be even younger than the twelve you accused me of being!'

He laughed, enjoying her rage. 'That annoyed you, did it?'

'Of course it did!' She was determined to remain lucid and intelligent, not to lose her cool again. 'And I'm surprised at a man of your obvious experience saying you don't see through either romance or sexual attraction. I should think you've had more than your fair share of relationships based on nothing but plain lust!'

He arched cool dark brows, revealing respect in his blue eyes at the direct honesty of her words. 'Clearly— so have you.'

'Of course I have.' She remained blindingly honest. 'I'm a young woman, I'm reasonably attractive, and I've had more than my fair share of men trying to seduce me.'

'Trying to?'

'Yes—*trying* to!'

'Obviously you never let them succeed.'

'Why should I?' Her face flushed unexpectedly. She felt defensive, lifting her chin. 'I have no intention of being hoodwinked by romantic delusion in order to let a man get the better of me sexually. That's what the game is, isn't it? That's how playboys reach their goal!'

He smiled, studying her assessingly. 'True, but not all men are playboys. You must have met at least one decent man since your husband died—surely? Or are you like most women, and find decent men boring?'

'They're certainly not as boring and predictable as playboys or fortune-hunters!'

'Fortune-hunters? A rich woman as well as a cynic, then?'

'Money and cynicism go hand in hand when everyone you meet just wants to relieve you of both your money and your virtue. And in truth I'd give all my money away to find one honest, decent, trustworthy man!'

'Then you do believe in love, after all.'

Her face flamed scarlet. 'No, I do not, and what is this anyway? Twenty questions? My private life is none of your damned business! Get off my back or I'll leave this yacht immediately!'

'OK.' He shrugged coolly, astonishing her while she stood there, bristling, poised for further fury, staring at him, a string of insults on the tip of her tongue—only to be completely outmanoeuvred because he strode mildly past them all, saying over one enormous bare, hard-muscled shoulder, 'I'm going into town for an hour or so. I'll see you all tonight. Seven-thirty on deck for cocktails...'

Speechless, furious, Emma stared after him as he picked up a nearby shirt, pulled it on lazily as he strode down the gangplank, and disappeared into the glamorous mêlée of people on the *quai* of St Tropez.

'That was Patrick doing the Spanish Inquisition, wasn't it?' Liz said as she too stared after Patrick. 'I wonder why?'

'He was probably just bored,' Emma said tersely, loathing him even more, and feeling shaken by the conversation. She decided she detested Patrick Kinsella, and would avoid him like the plague from now on. She turned to Liz, saying, 'I think I'd like to go down to my cabin now—take a shower, unpack, settle in. Would that be all right?'

'Yes, of course!' Liz put her drink down. 'See you later, Natasha.'

Natasha smiled acidly, said something spiteful, and refilled her glass while Liz led Emma along the hot wooden deck towards the white door which opened on to a long narrow staircase.

As they went down the stairs, Emma said tautly, 'Sorry about that row with your brother. I felt pinned down by all those questions, and the conversation was getting much too personal.'

'Oh, don't worry about it.' Liz waved an airy hand. 'He was obviously just intrigued to find a woman as cynical as he is.'

'Yes,' she said, eyes narrowing, 'I noticed his mad, bad and dangerous sex appeal before Natasha pointed it out. No doubt he's used to women falling at his feet in a romantic daydream.'

'Precisely,' Liz agreed. 'He stopped believing in love so long ago that I can't really remember a time when he wasn't a cynical swine.' She laughed, leading the way along a luxurious corridor. 'Not like me, of course, always rattling on about hearts and flowers.'

Emma smiled, following her past a series of doors. She liked Liz's preoccupation with romance, found it rather sweet, especially in the way it was expressed in her books—all that passion, faith in love, a belief in the goodness of people, not the bad.

It was a shame she had never married, but then she had had a ten-year blazing love-affair with a man who was married to an insane woman and felt unable to divorce her. 'All very Jane Eyre and Mr Rochester,' Liz often remarked with a sigh, but it had ended in tragedy when the man had died in a plane crash, leaving Liz alone in a world with no love but the romance in her beloved novels.

Liz opened the door of Emma's cabin, and smiled as she heard Emma's rapid intake of breath.

'My God, it's beautiful...!'

'Yes, my brother's very stylish in everything he does.'

Emma hated Patrick for being very stylish, but couldn't deny that he was, because this room was ravishing. It was vast, sunlight pouring in through two long windows, illuminating the sprawling silk-covered double bed, the deep-pile sea-green carpet, the expensive sofas and armchairs, the long low polished mahogany coffee-table, the antique writing-desk, and the exquisite paintings hanging on the silk-wallpapered walls.

'I'll leave you to get on with it, then,' said Liz with a cheery smile. 'See you at seven-thirty on deck for pre-dinner cocktails.'

As soon as the door was closed, Emma started to unpack, hanging all her clothes in the wardrobe, piling lingerie, T-shirts and jeans into the chest of drawers, and arranging her various shoes neatly.

Then she laid out her cosmetics, perfume and hair-styling appliances on the beautiful dressing-table, enjoying the reflection of that stylish bottle of Ralph Lauren's Safari in the three-tiered mirror.

Going into the bathroom with her toiletries, she gasped anew at the beauty, luxury and understated style of the room.

Patrick Kinsella really did have exceptional taste.

Taste meant a lot to Emma. Her late husband had had appalling taste, and living with it for the two years of their brief marriage had been very unpleasant. Another symptom of artifice and role-playing: Emma had let Simon indoctrinate her in everything he liked, as though she simply 'became' him, and pretended to like all his friends, his hobbies, his bad taste, his selfishness...

She had also, along the way, pretended to forgive him his brutality, violence, infidelity, deceit and vicious spite. All those qualities had only surfaced after the wedding—but then that was what you got, thought Emma, for pretending instead of telling the truth.

She wasn't bitter about the past, or about her bad marriage, or about the fact that she had been forced to role-play for so many years. She had dealt with it all long ago, accepting it and moving forward to a new life and a new way of dealing with the world.

What was there to do but forgive and, in doing so, forgive herself for the part she had played in her own unhappiness? Her parents had not loved her properly—but they had loved her, and she had loved them. It hadn't been their fault that they were so incapable of seeing her as she really was, it had simply been a product of their own unhappy childhoods, when their parents had not loved them properly.

As for Simon—well, he fell into the same category. Treated badly as a boy, he had grown up thinking that love meant treating other people badly, and his violence had been a product of long-buried rage.

Horrors.

What a minefield relationships were.

Now she was free of it all, content with her life, and looking back on the past was like looking back on another person. It would have been romantic of her to use the word 'rebirth' to describe her new life and, although she detested romance, she rather liked the word 'rebirth'.

Stripping her clothes off, she stepped into the luxurious shower, and proceeded to luxuriate under the warm needles of water, washing the grime of her long journey from her slender body.

To think she had left her London home at six o'clock this morning! God, that delay at London Heathrow had been a nightmare!

When she had dried herself, styled her hair, and pulled on a pair of pale blue jeans, she slipped a white silk top on, then decided it would be a shame to waste St Tropez if they were sailing out tonight, so she went up on deck with her sunglasses and handbag, and pootled down the gangplank into town.

Hot sunlight assailed her from all angles. Artists stood on the *quai* in front of their easels, palettes in hand as they stroked hot oil paints on to the canvases, and seagulls cried sharply among the bobbing boats, the glittering blue waters, the freedom-filled glamour of the town.

Emma walked lazily up bleached, winding, ancient streets, until she came to the main square, where old French men played *boules* among the trees and the dust, watched by glamorous tourists in pretty canopied cafés.

Sitting on a canvas chair, Emma watched the men, and ordered a coffee. Then suddenly, across the square, she saw a pair of blazing blue eyes watching her.

Dazzling blue, she thought again as she stared unsmilingly straight at Patrick Kinsella.

He just stood still, watching her, staring directly at her, and even though he was a long way away she felt the power of that stare, felt it very deeply, like a mirror turned in sudden blazing recognition.

She did not smile either. Nor make any attempt to wave or signal that she had seen him. Flicking her gaze expressionlessly from his, she glanced at the tree beside her as the warm breeze ruffled through its green leaves, and thought, Who the hell does he think he is?

When she glanced back with a cool expression, Patrick had gone. Frowning, she looked to see where he had disappeared to, but there was nothing there save the men playing *boules*, the trees, the dust, the cafés, and the sudden buzz of a motorbike driving along in the hot afternoon.

Oh, well. She shrugged philosophically, but it was irksome to have been stared at like that by her host, her employer's brother, as though he had no need to smile or wave or even acknowledge her.

What a sauce, she thought irritably. And after the way he spoke to me, asking me such rapid, personal questions. I may not be the best person he's ever invited aboard his yacht, but there's no need to completely ignore me in public, as though we've never met.

A second later, Liz appeared on the same side of the square as Emma.

'Hi!' Emma waved to her, and Liz waved back, looking hilarious in multi-stripe leggings, a long T-shirt and a bright orange baseball cap perched on her pixie-ish head.

'Hello there!' Liz raced over to her table, sank down in a chair and put her shopping down with a thud. 'Phew! This shopping is thirsty work! I must have a huge glass of Perrier.'

Emma signalled the waiter and ordered it for her.

'Settled in all right?' Liz asked.

'Yes, wonderfully well. I didn't want to waste St Tropez, though.' She hesitated, then, 'Just saw your brother, by the way, on the other side of the square.'

'And what did he have to say for himself? Anything interesting?'

'No, he didn't speak to me.' She sipped her coffee, still irritated by Patrick Kinsella's ignoring her.

'Didn't he? Maybe he didn't see you.'

'Yes, he did,' laughed Emma, 'but he was probably too busy eyeing up the other women in the cafés here to waste a smile on me!'

'He hardly needs to waste a smile on any woman,' sighed Liz. 'He's always had women flinging themselves at his feet—why should he bother to approach them?'

'Why indeed?' Emma said tightly. 'James Bond never has to do more than lift an eyebrow, and your brother seems to think he has a lot in common with James Bond, doesn't he?'

'Ouch!' Liz laughed. 'Poor Patrick! You really hate him, don't you?'

'One hundred per cent.'

'So there's no chance of you ever falling in love with him?'

Emma just laughed and shook her head.

Fall in love with him! The very idea . . .

CHAPTER TWO

EMMA dressed carefully that night, aware of the importance of first impressions, and aware that she didn't want either Toby or Charles, whom she had not yet met, to think she was a sexy woman up for grabs. Knowing Natasha just a little by now, she was fairly sure that Toby would have been told Emma was young, single and ready to mingle. I don't want to get grabbed, she thought, ready to spike Natasha's nasty little matchmaking guns.

The black evening dress she chose was serenely sensual, made of loose, elegant silk, making her look attractive without looking available. Pearls gleamed around her throat, pearl and diamond drops in her ears, glistening against the wealth of her long black curly hair. She wore strappy, black high heels, and was bathed in a discreet aura of Safari.

When she went up on deck, she steeled herself not only to spar with Natasha and meet the other two guests, but also to be very cool with the arrogant, conceited and thoroughly detestable Mr Patrick Kinsella.

To her annoyance, he was the only one there. Emma stopped on the tranquil deck, studying Patrick, who stood leaning against the steel railings looking out at St Tropez with his back to her. The sun glowed evening gold across the town, music came from the cafés opposite the yacht, and sports cars zoomed about, carrying breezy young people from lazy cafés to exclusive nightclubs. Patrick was wearing a black dinner-jacket, impeccably cut, and the way it fitted his powerful muscular body was pure poetry. Emma remembered Liz telling

23

her that women threw themselves at his feet and, looking
him up and down with dislike, she had to admit she could
see why. He wasn't her type, but as far as gorgeous
playboys were concerned he was a magnificent specimen.

He turned suddenly then and saw her. She found
herself momentarily breathless. His eyes were even more
blue, more dazzling, more acutely sensitive than she
remembered.

'Hi,' Emma said warily, and did not smile at him,
remembering his unsmiling stare in the leafy square of
the town and prickling under this latest, cool assessment.

'Hi.' He didn't smile either, but he did push lightly
away from the railings and lift his dark brows, saying,
'Do you want a drink?'

'Thanks.' She walked towards him, her heels click-
clacking elegantly on the wooden deck. 'Something light
and cold would be nice.'

Patrick moved like the giant he was to the table, and
poured a long cold drink for her. Emma watched his
body movements. He seemed at once fascinating and
loathsome. She wondered why. Then it occurred to her
that fascination and loathing were both intense reactions, which meant that she was far from indifferent to
him.

Emma was a great analyser of feelings. She had been
blinded too many times by emotions—powerful emotions, the kind that blistered and bludgeoned one's logic
into oblivion—and she had no intention of ever again
finding herself kneeling at the feet of some great male
god, who later turned out to be all too horribly human.

So recognising an emotional response to Mr Patrick
Kinsella was something which instantly sent her logic
into overdrive, demanding a rapid analysis of just *why*
she might react so strongly to him.

What had Liz told her about him? she wondered now
with narrowed, wary eyes. All she could remember was

that he was occasionally in the newspapers and that, in the past, he had been a notorious womaniser.

Work hard, play hard had been his motto, and the string of beauties his name had been linked with formed an impressive collection—film stars, beauty queens, models. He had hardly led a blameless life.

But lately, according to Liz, that aspect of his life had been played down in the Press because it had begun to affect his very serious reputation at work. All sex appeal aside, he was first and foremost a businessman, and he could hardly continue to live the life of James Bond without it rebounding on his business reputation. That didn't mean, however, that he no longer womanised. Far from it. He was probably just a lot more discreet. And that was further indication of quite how clever, calculating and cynical Patrick Kinsella really was.

'Here,' he said, and silver cuff-links flashed in his crisp white cuffs as he turned to hand her her drink. She thanked him with a polite smile, and for a second they drank in silence.

It was faintly uncomfortable. But Emma had no intention of making polite chit-chat with him, particularly after the way he'd behaved towards her so far.

Eventually, it was Patrick who broke the silence.

'Did you do any shopping in town?'

'Yes.' She sipped her drink and did not look at him.

'There are a number of very interesting shops here.'

'Yes, there are.' Emma nodded expressionlessly.

'My favourite is the tiny little art shop in the old part of town.'

Emma smiled politely and sipped her drink again. Patrick was silent for a moment, then came to loom next to her at the ship's railings. Emma pretended interest in the town. Patrick loomed. He was watching her. She felt acutely aware of his gaze and also aware of his anger.

Slowly, she looked up.

Their eyes met in a cool moment of mutual recognition.

He smiled slowly. So did she.

'We're going to be stuck on this yacht together,' drawled Patrick Kinsella, 'for another fortnight. Life will be so much easier if you don't bear a grudge.'

'I'm not bearing a grudge,' she drawled, just as cynical as he. 'I just respond to treatment, like any other normal human being.'

'And as my treatment of you thus far——' his hard mouth moved in a faint, rueful smile '—has hardly been exemplary, you intend to pay me back in kind. Is that it?'

'Precisely.'

'Because of our discussion this afternoon?'

'I felt attacked, Mr Kinsella. Didn't you notice?'

'I thought you could take it.'

'I can take it. But every action has a reaction.'

'And this is yours? Hmm. Well, that's something I can take, too. Besides, you were patronising all of us with what you were saying.'

'Oh, was I?'

'Yes, you were.' His blue eyes were as direct as his words. 'You thought we were all arguing for romance. You thought you were talking to a bunch of naïve teenagers still living in bluebird-and-orange-blossom land.'

'I can assure you,' she laughed cynically, 'I would never put you in that particular category!'

'Better not, Miss Baccarat. I stopped believing in romance a long time ago.'

'I don't doubt it,' she said, eyeing him with cat-like suspicion. 'I had you pegged for an arrogant, cynical swine as soon as I saw you.'

He laughed. 'Good for you.' The blue eyes danced with rakish amusement as he looked down his arrogant nose at her. 'Honest as well as beautiful.'

'Flattery won't work with me.'

'It's not flattery. You are honest—and beautiful. I didn't notice it when you first boarded. You just seemed like another pretty little dolly in a red dress. But dollies don't have serious integrity, and you do appear to have, even if it is a little misguided.'

'Forgive a mere dolly having the presumption to ask, but how can integrity be misguided?'

'Because it misses the mark.'

'And what particular mark might that be?'

His brows arched. 'The truth.'

Emma smiled through her perfect white teeth. 'You're very patronising.'

'Am I?'

'I fear so. But don't let it worry you. I fully intend to patronise you into the ground before this cruise is out.'

He laughed again, eyes smiling into hers as he leant idly beside her, tall and handsome and well aware of it. 'Well, that's what you were doing this afternoon. That's why I broke in and stopped you pussyfooting around. You're so used to being with people who still live in fairyland that you automatically feed them palliatives instead of saying what you really think.'

'There's no point in trying to destroy their illusions, Mr Kinsella. They wouldn't listen even if you did try.'

'Well, I won't argue with that. You have to leave them wandering blindfold through a maze, bumping into things, never recognising them for what they are, labouring under the delusions of love, romance, happy-ever-after...' He laughed harshly and shook his dark head. 'It's enough to make one horribly cynical.'

She laughed too, green eyes blazing with a strange mixture of dislike, admiration and understanding. 'But you are horribly cynical.'

'So I am!' He laughed then, but as the breeze gently played with his jet-black hair his smile faded and he drawled, 'It's very isolating, isn't it?'

'Yes, it is.'

They seemed to have reached a point of mutual agreement without realising it, and Emma didn't stop to think about what she said next, because it just seemed like a natural progression of the conversation, which she thought was still an argument.

'I often wonder,' she said, 'if I'll ever be able to be completely honest with another human being, because everyone I meet always tries to persuade me that black is white and white is black.'

'Like addicts trying to get you hooked on their particular drug.' He nodded coolly, unsmiling. 'Religion isn't the opium of the masses any more—romantic love is. And, as with all drugs, once the haze clears, one cannot tolerate real life. One has a clear-cut choice: take some more of the drug, or face reality.'

Emma shuddered. 'I prefer reality.'

'Me too.' He studied her with a smile. 'But, as you so rightly said, one despairs of ever finding someone with whom one can be completely honest. It's as though everybody else is living on another planet. I used to find it depressing, but I'm so used to feeling isolated from the people I love that I——' He broke off suddenly, staring at her, then gave a slow smile, looking right into her eyes with a frown, and drawled sardonically, 'What an extraordinary conversation!'

The sea breeze flickered through Emma's hair as she smiled at him, thinking the same thing.

Patrick gave a cool, wry laugh. 'What made me tell you all of that?'

'I don't know.' Emma smiled lazily at him. 'I'm just wondering the same thing myself, about what I told you.'

'Most embarrassing,' he drawled with a rakish laugh. 'Let's not tell anyone we had this conversation!'

'Agreed!'

'Shake on it.'

Their hands moved out, touched, clung.

Suddenly, a peculiar silence descended on them, one of deep intimacy, respect and mutual understanding. Emma's toes curled. Her hand was in his and she just kept smiling, felt her heart begin to beat faster. He smiled too, eyes glittering down into hers, then, very slowly, he stopped smiling, and as he did she felt her heart thud, her body jump as though energised by some unstoppable force, and her eyes drop like fire to his hard, handsome mouth.

When she looked up she saw that he was staring at her mouth too. His gaze flashed up suddenly to meet hers. Their hands tightened together, and the unexpected violence of sexual attraction reared up between them so powerfully that Emma felt her whole body shake with it.

'Ahoy there!' Liz called cheerily from along the deck.

Patrick and Emma leapt away from each other as though burnt—or as though they'd been caught in some illicit, deeply intimate act.

'Where are all the others?' Liz tottered towards them in a peacock-blue silk dress, high heels and a cloud of Joy perfume. 'Don't tell me Charles and Toby are *still* in town!'

'No, they came back to the ship at around six...'

Emma struggled for composure as Patrick talked to his sister, but she was deeply shaken, and so was her body—her heart was pounding much too fast, her pulses racing like wildfire, and the tension suddenly coiling in her stomach was at once frightening and exciting.

Stupid, she said to herself, sipping her drink too quickly, alarmed by the tremor of her hands. We were only talking. No need to get so pathetically romantic about it all of a sudden, as though I genuinely wanted to kiss him.

Of course I don't want to kiss him, she thought, and stared at his firm, handsome, sexy mouth.

'So,' said Liz with a smile, 'what have you two been talking about up here on your own?'

Emma's eyes met Patrick's in a fierce blaze of mutual understanding. She looked away quickly, but not before she had noticed how very handsome his face was, the tough bones beneath the tanned skin strikingly male, revealing a formidable personality in the hard, sensual set of his mouth, the uncompromising line of his jaw, and the sexy droop of those heavy eyelids.

He's quite superb, she thought with a shock as she heard her voice say with false gaiety, 'Oh, we were just talking about St Tropez.'

Patrick shot her a quick, unsmiling stare that made her blush. She had lied. Why had she lied? She couldn't understand it.

'Good old St Tropez!' Liz was pouring herself a drink. 'Patrick, did you tell her how many times you've been here?'

'Yes, I did,' Patrick lied, and now it was her turn to stare at him. He looked away from her, raking a hand through his jet-black hair. She saw him raise his glass to his mouth, take a drink, then look back at her with a hard, narrowed stare that focused on her eyes, then on her mouth, then moved slowly down her body in a rapid, unsmiling assessment, as though he had only just noticed her body—but how he noticed it now, in every detail, fast, fast, fast, whizzing over the curve of her full breasts, the narrow slenderness of her waist, down past her slim hips and on down over her legs—long, shapely legs—right down to her narrow ankles.

'I love St Tropez.' Liz was oblivious to their silent intimacy. 'It's such a beautiful place, full of so many...'

Patrick's eyes met Emma's suddenly, and the dark, dangerous desire she saw revealed in them made her want to run screaming from this sunlit deck.

'Oh, look!' Liz broke off her rhapsody of St Tropez. 'Here come good old Toby and Charles!'

Emma dragged her hectic gaze from Patrick's, breathing in shallow, inaudible little gasps as she struggled to come to terms with what she was feeling—and what he was so obviously feeling too. She told herself it couldn't possibly be real. It must be some kind of mistake or accident. After all, nobody really felt physical attraction so powerfully. That was just something that happened in storybooks, films, romantic novels.

'Evening all!' called a jolly, boyish blond man in his mid-thirties. 'Crack open the champers! I've arrived!'

'Hi, Toby!' Liz went to greet him with a kiss. 'You're looking awfully flushed! You must have caught the sun this afternoon!'

'I always do. It's the de Courcey skin. I think one of our ancestors must have been old Dracula himself.'

Emma was acutely aware of Patrick standing close to her, watching her with his heavy-lidded eyes. He was leaning against the rails, one strong hand close to the small of her back, and all she could think about was how close it was, and how very easily it could slide up on to her back, those long fingers moving lightly over her skin...

'Toby, have you met my friend Emma Baccarat?'

'No, but I can't wait to do so! Look at that stunning figure!'

Emma smiled politely, shook his hand, aware of Patrick's blue eyes on her, and of the long hand so close to her back.

'What a cracker you are!' Toby giggled. 'Why didn't anyone tell me the new arrival was so gorgeous?'

Everyone laughed.

'And have you met our cousin Charles?' Liz was gesturing to the tall, elegant blond man who was with Toby. 'He's married to Natasha.'

'The Wicked Witch of the West,' Toby said, giggling.

'Don't be horrible about my poor darling Natasha,' said Charles.

Emma barely noticed either Toby or Charles. She was too busy noticing Patrick Kinsella, standing beside her, stunningly gorgeous, unbearably handsome, frighteningly real...

'How do you do, Miss Baccarat?' Charles de Courcey said with infinite charm, shaking her hand, his dark eyes gentle and sweet.

'Very well, thank you.' Emma shook his hand and wished Patrick would disappear. 'And you?'

'Oh, marvellous. Had a lovely day; looks like it's going to be a super night...'

Patrick finished his drink, moved with cool male grace to the table, put his glass down. Emma didn't look at him but she saw every move he made, every ripple of muscle beneath that impeccable black dinner-jacket, every turn of his dark head and every flicker of his blue, blue eyes.

'Uh-oh!' Toby giggled suddenly. 'Here comes The Evil One.'

Natasha appeared on deck looking drop-deadly in a shimmering silver sheath which she must have been poured into, for it clung to her every slender curve. Her dark hair was pushed back in a sultry swath, her heavy eyelids were outlined in black and her lips dripped blood-red gloss.

'Vampirella, I presume!' Toby joked.

'Do be quiet, Toby,' Natasha said, slinking towards them. 'Don't give Charles a drink, Patrick—he's been knocking back the sherry all afternoon, and I don't want him to lose consciousness too soon. Why, Miss Baccarat! Weren't you told to dress for dinner?'

Emma barely registered the insult—she was too busy forcing herself not to feel what she was feeling.

'I think Emma looks absolutely superb,' Patrick murmured coolly, watching her from beneath those heavy eyelids and making her heart skip rapid beats.

'Well, you would, Patrick!' Natasha said waspishly. 'No doubt you've decided to take up the challenge. After all, if anyone can get Miss Baccarat to fall wildly in love, it's you.'

Emma stiffened like a board, her hand clutching her glass so tightly, she thought it might shatter into a thousand pieces. Over my dead body! she told herself furiously. Over my dead body!

'What's that supposed to mean?' asked Toby.

'Oh, we were having this conversation when they first arrived...' said Natasha, but Emma wasn't listening— she was furiously remembering Patrick's reputation as a lady-killer, playboy, seducer *par excellence*. She felt a fool, humiliated, aware now that Patrick Kinsella had probably elicited these responses in her through experience or cynical manipulation or some other technique which she had no defence against.

I knew they weren't real feelings, she thought angrily, sipping her drink too fast. I knew feelings like these didn't exist outside storybooks.

'...and she said she didn't believe in love or romance.'

Emma's face was burning angry crimson. She didn't know where to look or what to say. She wanted to die.

'So I told her she *must* want someone to kiss from time to time...'

Patrick moved coolly, suddenly, and as his powerful body blocked the others from her view Emma looked up into his clever, serious eyes and felt breathless all over again because he clearly understood what was going on inside her mind. She swallowed hard, dragging her gaze from his. He hesitated for a second, then his long fingers touched her cheek, making her quite literally catch her breath and stare up at him again, horrified.

'... and then Patrick asked her if she'd ever wanted to kiss anyone...'

Emma looked down suddenly at his mouth, then went scarlet, felt more vulnerable than she had ever felt in her life, and had no option other than to bend her dark head because there was nowhere else to hide.

Turning from Emma, Patrick cut into Natasha's diatribe. 'I think it's time we all left for dinner.'

They all turned to look up at him, as though he were a god.

'I booked the table for eight o'clock, and it's nearly that now.' He studied the black and silver Rolex on his wrist, the crisp white cuff shooting back to reveal a tanned, black-haired forearm. 'As we have to sail at midnight, I think an early start is advisable.'

They left the yacht, a glamorous set of people bathed in gold evening light, walking along the expensive shopping streets while open-topped sports cars zoomed past and little red Lambretta scooters whizzed along carrying young people in jeans, their hair blowing back in the hot breeze.

Naturally, they fell into pairs as they walked. Charles and Toby. Natasha and Liz...

Patrick fell into step beside Emma. She felt her heart beating too fast. The warm sun was on her skin, the breeze in her hair, and all the lights of St Tropez seemed bright, hot, blazing with glamour.

'Do you think you'll enjoy the cruise?'

It was small talk, and Emma was grateful for that, answering, 'Yes. Particularly Morocco. I've never been there.'

'Rabat is very beautiful.' His voice was deep, cool, very male. 'It's the capital, but it's quite a way inland from Casablanca, which is where we'll be stopping. I'll hire a car, drive you into the city for——'

'No, that's quite all right!' Emma tried hard not to sound as though she was afraid of spending an entire day alone with him, although she had a sneaking suspicion that she was. 'Casablanca will be fine for me. I don't need to see Rabat.'

He just looked at her coolly, analytically, from under those heavy eyelids, and her heart skipped so many beats she was surprised she didn't have a cardiac arrest.

'How much longer till we get to this restaurant?' she demanded with a brittle laugh, and then blushed hotly, aware of his serious blue eyes burning through her pretence. 'I'm really quite hungry!'

He looked at her in cool enquiry, and his eyes wanted to know why she was resorting to such artifice.

Feeling sick, she looked away from him.

'Here we are!' Natasha said suddenly, stopping at a vast restaurant surrounded by black iron grilles, plants and flowers and trees in the garden beneath the long blue and white canopy. 'Well done, Patrick! You unerringly pick the most exclusive restaurants.'

He gave a cool, wry smile. 'Just for you, Natasha,' he said, and pushed open the gate of the private enclosure, watching Emma as she walked past him, making her very aware of his every look, his every flicker of thought.

The *maître d'* swept up to them, bowed low. 'Monsieur Kinsella! How wonderful to see you again! May I show you to your table...?'

Emma walked with the others across the terracotta paving. Women stared at Patrick in open admiration, men with jealous awe.

'He looks like one of your heroes, doesn't he?' Natasha said to Liz. 'Tall, dark and dangerous.'

Emma pretended not to hear. Dry-mouthed, she wandered aimlessly around while the others took their places. Patrick sat at the head of the table, leaning back coolly, his powerful eyes watching her trying to sit as far away from him as possible.

'Oh, are you sitting up here with me?' Toby said in surprise as she sat down beside him, in the furthest chair from Patrick. 'I thought you were getting on famously with Patrick?'

'Well, I just ended up walking with him, that's all.' She smiled, aware of Patrick's laser-blue eyes burning on her, and deliberately did not look in his direction, smiling instead at Toby. 'And now I've ended up sitting with you.'

'Good-oh!' Toby giggled amiably. 'What shall we talk about? Oh—I know! Let's talk about sex! That's always a good dinner party conversation!'

'Trust Toby to lower the moral tone,' Natasha said contemptuously. 'I say—is that Brigitte Bardot over there?'

Everybody looked to see if it was.

The waiter came up to take their order. Emma decided on sole *meunière* with salad because she had a feeling she was losing her appetite, and didn't want everyone to notice—especially not Patrick.

'I must remember to use this restaurant in one of my books,' Liz said when the waiter had gone. 'It's a great place for the hero to take the heroine. They could have that corner table over there and argue passionately over their main course.'

'Why do they always have to argue?' Natasha asked.

'Because,' said Liz, 'when two people fall in love they invariably fight tooth and claw to stop it happening.'

Emma slowly leaned her head to one side to look at Patrick while he wasn't looking at her. She knew he couldn't be looking at her, because she could hear him talking to Charles, but she was mistaken—he was looking straight at her, and as their eyes collided she felt so violently exposed that it was like being staked stark naked to her chair.

'Usually, though,' said Liz, sipping her wine, 'the man recognises it first and acts on it.'

Emma dragged her gaze from Patrick's and stared at the crystal glass in front of her.

'But it's all tied up with sexual attraction, you see, especially for him,' Liz went on. 'So he just keeps trying to get the heroine into bed, and, of course, she reacts like a scalded cat, because she thinks that's all he wants.'

'It usually is,' said Natasha.

Patrick's blue eyes flicked briefly, hotly, to Emma's breasts.

'And that's why they argue so much,' Liz said. 'It's the age-old difference between the sexes.'

'Men want sex and women want love?' Natasha laughed. 'Stale news!'

'So the minute the man pounces on the woman,' said Liz, 'all hell breaks loose because he can't admit his feelings and she can't let him make love to her until he does. Stalemate. Somebody has to give.'

Patrick Kinsella looked directly at Emma, his face hard, handsome, very cool, and as she met his eyes she felt devoid of all defence, completely convinced that he could see the bare vulnerability in her face, her skin, her hands, her shoulders, the very set of her body.

Pull yourself together! she thought furiously, and looked down at her knife and fork. Her hands shook as she blindly rearranged them.

'Oh, look!' said Natasha. 'Miss Baccarat's gone all shaky!'

Emma flicked angry green eyes up to her spiteful face. 'I'm tired. I should have slept instead of going shopping.'

'Not all this talk about passionate lovers, then?' Natasha laughed. 'You must be getting quite desperate now that you're twenty-six, mustn't you? Speaking of desperate—where the hell is my lobster? I'm starving.'

'Desperate?' said Toby with a laugh. 'Who, this little beauty? She's the most gorgeous thing I've seen in years. In fact I'm surprised Patrick hasn't commented on her stunning looks. He's usually the fastest gun in the West when it comes to seducing a pretty lady.'

Emma's mouth tightened and she steeled herself not to look at Patrick.

'But then he's so discreet,' said Toby, 'that he's probably planning to come to your cabin later tonight and relieve you of your négligé.'

Patrick's dark lashes flickered and a faint smile touched his hard, sensual mouth. He shot a quick, lazy, burning look at Emma that told her Toby had hit the nail right on the head.

That was exactly what he had been planning to do.

Over my dead body, thought Emma furiously, glaring at him. Over my dead body!

CHAPTER THREE

THE ship sailed at midnight.

Emma stood on deck, leaning on the railings, her hair flickering gently in the breeze as the yacht motored out of harbour. The sky was black, pin-pricked by stars, and St Tropez looked beautiful as it got further away in the distance, that little cluster of bleached buildings still lit up in gold, villas dotted on the dark hills around, and lights winking up and down the night-time coast of the Gulf of St Tropez.

Patrick was standing coolly on the other side of the deck, talking to Liz in a deep, murmuring voice. Emma was aware of his every move although she did not look at him once.

'We'll be in Málaga tomorrow lunchtime,' Toby said, drinking a glass of champagne. 'It's the perfect place for lazy tourists.'

'To be honest,' Emma replied, 'Málaga doesn't really interest me. I'd much rather go to Granada. I thought I could hire a car...'

'Oh, don't be boring!' Toby laughed. 'Spend the day in Málaga with me. Go on. We are both young, single and gorgeous!'

Emma laughed wryly, caught the turn of Patrick's head, saw the narrowing of his tough blue eyes, and knew not only that he had overheard Toby's gentle pass at her, but had not liked it.

'Besides,' said Toby, putting an arm around her slim shoulders, 'we're stuck together on this yacht for the next fortnight. We may as well make the most of it...'

Emma instinctively slithered out of Toby's embrace. Years of practice made her appear to brush him away affectionately, a smile in her eyes and warmth in her body. The perfect rejection of an unwanted advance. And Patrick Kinsella noted it with cynical amusement from the other side of the deck.

'Speaking of getting used to this cruise,' Emma said lightly as she moved completely away from Toby, 'I'm exhausted. All that travelling! Would anyone mind if I went straight down to bed?'

'No, of course not, Emma!' Toby tried to kiss her goodnight.

'Night night!' she said lightly, slithering artfully away from him and his kiss.

Patrick's eyes glinted as he watched her across the deck, but he said nothing, and as everyone else chorused their goodnights to her she went downstairs to her cabin.

The motion of the ship was strange at first, making her clutch the banister on the stairs as they swayed faintly this way and that. The wood was creaking slightly, the throb of the engines was oddly comforting, and she certainly felt a lot better moving into the privacy of her cabin after an entire nerve-racking evening with Patrick Kinsella around.

Once inside her cabin, she undressed, pulled on her black silk pyjamas, took off her make-up and brushed out her long curly black hair.

It was warm, private, something of a sanctuary with such low lighting, and as she slid in between the soft, clean sheets she was already feeling sleepy. Plunging out the lights, she buried her head on the fat pillows and closed her eyes. What exactly was going on—if anything—with Patrick? This deep physical attraction, this overwhelming awareness—how on earth had it sprung up so unexpectedly between them?

The answer was fairly obvious, in truth—Patrick had manufactured it by working some peculiar kind of magic on her. He was very practised at seduction. She might be cynical and aware of the dangers, but that didn't mean she was immune, especially to the charms of a clever womaniser.

Still vulnerable after all these years, she thought with a sigh, and closed her eyes, vowing just to ignore her inexplicable feelings for Patrick, regardless of how much magic he managed to work on her during this cruise.

The ship swayed this way and that. They were out of the gulf now, steaming across the Med towards the Spanish coast, and as they negotiated bigger waves the walls creaked more heavily, until the sound of the engines, the creaking of the walls and the gentle motion of the yacht became something of a lullaby, and she fell asleep.

Sleep, sleep, sleep . . .

She dreamed deeply.

She was in her parents' house, and she was eighteen again. The doorbell rang. She ran to answer the door, ran outside, and found herself surrounded by a sunlit forest. When she turned around, the house had vanished. All that was left was her bed, in the middle of the sunlit forest clearing, and Patrick Kinsella was sitting on the bed, waiting for her, just watching her in silence.

Emma woke up with a stifled gasp.

The cabin was in pitch-darkness, the walls were creaking, and somebody was sitting on her bed.

She punched on the light with a cry of horror.

Patrick shielded his eyes; so did she.

'What are you doing in here?' she said hoarsely, clutching at the duvet, her heart pounding fifty million beats per minute.

'God, that light's bright!' His voice was deep as he let his hand fall, eyes narrowed.

He still wore his black trousers, but the jacket had been discarded, and so had the tie. His white shirt was unbuttoned at the throat: she could see the black hairs on his chest and the powerful muscles below.

'Just answer my question, Patrick!' Emma said. 'What are you *doing* here, alone in my bedroom with me——' she glanced hectically at her watch '—at two o'clock in the morning?'

'I couldn't sleep.'

'That's not a good enough reason.'

'I wanted to see you.'

Breathless, she looked away, muttering huskily, 'That's...not a good reason either.' Now how had her voice come out sounding husky?

Patrick gave her a cool, charming smile. 'Are you going to tell me you didn't notice anything odd happening tonight between us?'

'No.' She felt her face burning red, her heart banging loudly. 'Nothing at all.'

His smile mocked her. 'So why did you avoid me all night?'

'I didn't.'

'Yes, you did.'

'No, I didn't.'

His hand caught her chin in a sudden angry vice-like grip with long fingers, forcing her to look at him, his blue eyes glittering. 'I think you did, Emma!'

She stared up at him, her heart hammering insanely, and felt unable to think of a reply. Denying it wouldn't help, and there was little chance of slithering successfully away from him in these circumstances—she was alone in bed and he was stronger than she was. Slithering was definitely out of the question.

'No clever come-back?' His dark brows arched with amusement.

'Give me a minute,' she muttered huskily. 'I'll think of one.' She hated the way her voice kept going husky all of a sudden. She had had no idea that her voice contained that particular quality or tone. 'Meanwhile I'd be grateful if you'd let go of me and get out of my cabin!'

'And I'd be grateful if you'd tell me the truth.'

She couldn't look at him. 'What truth?'

'The truth you're avoiding with your eyes right now.'

She stared fixedly at a point just above the open neck of his white shirt, refusing to meet his eyes, aware that if she did he would bend his dark head and kiss the living daylights out of her.

'What a little coward you are!' Patrick murmured tauntingly. 'So much for Emma Baccarat, the soul of integrity, the woman who can tell the difference between romance and sexual attraction!'

'I *can* tell the difference! That's why I want you to get off my bed and out of my cabin immediately!'

'Because you're scared of the attraction between us?'

'That's right!'

'But I thought you said nothing was happening between us?'

She caught her breath, staring directly into his eyes and feeling pinned down through the centre of the heart by the hard black pupils surrounded by all that steely, stunning blue.

'I think you should leave,' she said huskily.

'I don't want to leave. I want to kiss you.'

Her heart raced like mad. 'Oh, God...'

'That's what I was thinking, all night, every time I looked at you.'

'Don't——'

'Or didn't you notice I couldn't take my eyes off you?'

'I've had enough of this!' She tried to push him away and get out of the bed, but he stopped her, staring down at her, and for a second she was motionless.

Then he suddenly lowered his dark head.

She caught her breath, struggled wildly, but he was insistent, and even though he was a giant, bigger and stronger than she was, he was surprisingly gentle as he forced her, completely against her will, to accept his kiss.

The cabin was punctuated with sounds of their tussle: the sheets rustling, the light thud against the wall, the gasps from her mouth as she tried to evade him.

Then suddenly, as though a switch had been thrown, she felt a rush of desire so powerful that she moaned, let her lips part just for a second, felt his tongue slip through to meet hers, and a second later she was kissing him back with an answering passion that appalled her as much as it excited her.

His prey surrendering briefly, Patrick moved like lightning. He pushed her back on to the pillows, almost clumsy in his haste. They fell together awkwardly, and she tried to sit up again, murmuring, 'No,' against his hot mouth, but he was quick, very quick, his lips opening hers beneath him as one strong hand tunnelled into the wealth of her dark hair, making her helpless as her arms wrapped themselves around his neck and the kiss took fire.

Her head spun dizzily. She could barely breathe. Her excitement was so violent, so unprecedented and so out of the blue that all she could do was kiss, be kissed, lose herself in his mouth, his arms, his touch, his scent...

'Yes...!' Patrick said thickly, and fumbled with one hand to punch out the light. Darkness fell between them and, as it did, so Emma's fear slipped away under a tidal wave of unprecedented hunger, making it easy, so easy to drown in his kiss, the touch of his hands, the completely natural feel of it all...

Her mouth drank thirstily from his. She felt as though they had entered a completely different dimension. It was as though a door had opened between them when they'd talked together earlier today, and that Patrick had just walked through it to claim her forever.

Forever lay in this kiss. Forever...

This is insane, she thought wildly. Why am I thinking such crazy, romantic, stupid, *stupid* thoughts?

She started to fight, aware even as she pushed at his powerful chest that she loved the feel of it, wanted to undress him, be naked with him, make absolute love with him and lose herself in his body.

'Don't, don't, don't...!' her swollen mouth muttered against his, and he stopped, raising his head an inch from hers, dragging air into his lungs. 'Please!'

His face was flushed in the darkness. 'Are you all right?'

'No, I'm not all right!' Her voice shook. 'I don't like this at all and I want it to stop happening!'

'I don't think it's going to, but I certainly agree we should talk before we go any further.'

'What do you mean, go any further? You don't seriously think this is going to lead to sex, do you? You do! I can see it in your eyes! My God, get off this bed before I——'

'I think we need to talk—that's all.'

'Not like this, not on my bed, not in the dark!'

He breathed harshly for a moment in silence, then slowly reached out one hand to punch the light back on. It flooded the cabin, blinding them both once more.

For a second, Emma just lay there staring up at his hard, handsome face, seeing the dark colour on his cheekbones, the fierce heat of his blue eyes, the tousled black hair where her own fingers had run so passionately through it.

Then she pushed back the duvet and tried to get out of bed.

He stopped her at once, his hands gripping her slim shoulders.

'Take your hands off me!' she whispered fiercely, and he didn't move for a second, but he saw the fierce glare of her eyes, glittering like savage emeralds in her flushed face. His dark lashes flickered. He released her, lowered his gaze, and she scrambled off the bed in a breathless movement, black silk pyjamas rippling on her slender body.

Putting a hand to her forehead, she moved to the windows, breathing in shallow, inaudible gasps. She pulled the curtain back a little, staring out at the dark, moonlit sea as they sailed on through the night.

She didn't know what to say to him. What could she possibly say?

Patrick watched her from the bed for a moment, then said deeply, 'I could get some drinks for us both. The night staff will bring us——'

'I just want you to leave, Patrick.'

'I think that would be a mistake.'

She laughed unsteadily.

'I'm serious.' He got to his feet, strode coolly up behind her, making her whirl round, her heart banging hard, feeling even smaller now in bare feet, confronted by his extreme and unbelievable height, staring up into his eyes with obvious alarm. 'This is a good chance for us to discuss what's happening. And don't look at me like that. You know as well as I do that something's going on.'

'No, I don't, Patrick!'

'How can you say that?'

'Because it's true!'

'After the way you just kissed me, the way——'

'Look.' She was flustered, defensive. 'I don't want to talk to you. I don't want to feel any of this. I don't want to——'

'Oh, you admit you *do* feel it, then? Well, at least we're making some kind of progress.'

'All right, yes, I admit I feel it!' Angrily she pushed past him, unable to bear the horrific awareness, the leaping of her blood, the burning, insistent excitement in her groin. 'But I don't want to!' She walked over to the couch but did not sit down on it, just turned in front of it to look at him across the low-lit room. 'I didn't want to in the first place, and I have no intention of allowing it to continue. We don't know each other, we only just met, and all this is so utterly absurd that I'm astonished that two grown-up people are giving it any credence whatever!'

'I think only grown-up people *could* give it credence.'

'In other words—let's be adult about this?' Her eyes blazed with angry resentment. 'Yes, that's a good line, Patrick, but I've heard it so many times before that it's somehow lost its impact!' She watched him warily across the room. 'I know what's supposed to follow it, you see. Not that it's ever happened to me, because it hasn't. But it has happened to a lot of my girlfriends. It's usually either a playboy or a married man who says it, and what he really means is, Let's have gratuitous casual sex!'

'That isn't what I was asking for, Emma.'

'Then what was all that about, just a moment ago, on my bed?'

'You tell me. You were participating.'

Her face flushed betrayingly. She felt embarrassed and lowered her head, the tousled silk of her dark hair sliding over the heat of her cheeks.

'Emma——' his voice was deep as he watched her '—you know as well as I do that there's a fierce physical attraction between us. But there's a lot more to it than that.'

She tensed, didn't look at him, trying to appear cool. 'Such as?'

'I don't know. I'm not sure. I just like your mind, the way you think, the way you talk.'

'Not just a pretty little dolly after all, then,' she said sarcastically. 'I wonder if there's a string in the middle of my back? When you pull it, interesting words come out.'

He laughed, blue eyes dancing.

'Look...' She shifted stance, studying him through her lashes. 'I just came on holiday, that's all. I wanted to see Morocco and Madeira. Sunbathe, relax, and spend some time with new people. The last thing I expected was to be swept away on a tide of complete insanity.'

'It was the last thing I expected, too.'

Her heart skipped a sickening beat.

'But I'm not a coward, Emma. I face things when they hit me and deal with them immediately. I certainly don't run like a rabbit the way you're trying to.'

Angrily, she met his gaze. 'I am *not* running like a rabbit!'

'Then what are you doing?' He walked towards her with a rapid stride, aware that she was tempted to back, to run and prove his accusation of cowardice, and it was only because of that that she stood her ground, heart banging violently, refusing to do what every instinct screamed at her to do: run and keep running.

'I'm trying to keep this under control,' she heard her voice say with that inexplicable female huskiness. 'If you're sensible, you'll agree that by this time tomorrow we won't feel it any more.'

'You think not?' He stopped in front of her.

'I'm sure of it.'

'Just a temporary aberration, then?'

'Well, what else can it be?' She stared into his eyes and felt as though she was in a lift dropping seventy-five floors in two seconds. Their eyes seemed to lock and hold as though there were no barriers between their two minds, as though doors were opening faster than she could cope with, as though they were fusing together.

'No.' She dragged her gaze from his, scared out of her wits, her voice unbearably husky, unbearably emotional, unbearably female. 'On seconds thoughts, don't answer that. I don't want to hear what you think. I just want you to go away.'

'Because you're afraid of the way you feel?'

'Why shouldn't I be afraid of it?' Her eyes flared suddenly. 'I only met you today. All I know about you is that you're a womaniser, and here I am alone in my bedroom with you trying to seduce me! I'd be a complete idiot if I wasn't afraid!'

'Point taken. OK. Let's be a little more civilised about this, then. Let's just sit down on the couch for a second and try to talk it over.'

'Lull me into a false state of security before pouncing on me again? Very clever, Patrick. One problem. I have no intention of being lulled into anything.'

'Hey—I promise not to touch you. I just want to talk.'

He sounded so sincere that she almost believed him. But all wolves sound sincere, she reminded herself angrily, and he's no different from the rest.

'Emma,' he said deeply, 'I give you my word that I won't touch you.'

She hesitated, green eyes wary as a cornered cat's.

As though to move things along a little, Patrick sank down, leaning back, watching her as she stood there in her black silk pyjamas. That couch was just as dangerous as the bed, in truth. He could just as easily get her in a horizontal position on that, and her skin screamed with mad, inexplicable desire at the thought of how it would feel to lie against his hard body.

'Come on.' His long fingers slid over her wrist, pulling her down on to the couch beside him.

She landed with a light thud, heart beating fast, watching him through her lashes. 'You said you wouldn't touch me.'

'I'm not.' He smiled slowly, eyes gleaming. 'Just my hand on your wrist. An everyday sort of touch—don't you think?'

'It doesn't feel everyday to me.'

'Nor me,' he agreed softly. 'But that's because we're both in the grip of the most insane desire that I've ever felt.'

Her heart raced violently but she couldn't bring herself to deny it. Not this close, not while she was looking directly into those dazzling, powerful, intelligent blue eyes.

'It is insane, Patrick. That's why I'm not going to let you sate it with me.'

He slowly linked his long fingers with hers. 'Perhaps not.'

'It's not what I want, Patrick.' She forced herself to be honest because the linking of his fingers with hers was making her melt inside with overwhelming emotion and desire. 'I admit I want you to kiss me. I admit I thought about little else all night. But I didn't have wild fantasies of lovemaking or——'

'That's because you're a woman,' he drawled. 'You'll begin by seeing nothing but the kiss because it's the way nature programmed you.'

'Really?' Her eyes flashed angrily. 'And I'll eventually get to your particular stage of seeing nothing but the full *son et lumière*, will I? Don't bank on it!'

'You want me, Emma.' He studied her directly. 'I knew it before I kissed you, but I know it doubly now.'

Her face burned. 'Fine! Know it as much as you like! But you're not going to get it, so why keep on trying to talk me into it?'

'I told you before—there's something a lot more powerful than just physical desire going on between us, and I'm prepared to pursue that.' He gave a sardonic laugh, eyes glittering. 'I won't deny that I have every intention of trying to make love to you for as long as I can be this close to you, but it's not the most important thing on my mind.'

She studied him in fearful excitement. 'Then what is?'

He was silent for a moment, watching her, then said coolly, 'That isn't something I'm prepared to discuss.'

'No, because you're an expert from way back, and you figure the best way into a woman's bed is to trap her with romance when all you want is sex!'

'But if you don't believe in romance, how can I trap you with it?' He studied her coolly, and his silence made her aware of her constricted breathing, the violent pounding of her heart, and the burning of her skin.

'At any rate,' she said unsteadily, 'I think this conversation has gone quite far enough. It's very late, we both have to sleep, and I'd like you to go now. OK?'

He just looked at her, those blue eyes filled with desire, and as she met his gaze she felt as though she'd been kicked in the stomach at close range.

'Don't look at me like that, Patrick!' Her voice shook with defensive anger.

Slowly, he leaned towards her, slid one hand on to her white throat, making her shiver from head to foot with such delicious response that her toes curled, her nipples became erect, and fire began to burn her skin.

'Don't . . .' she whispered thickly.

He bent his dark head to blot out the light as he kissed her.

She struggled hard, once, twice, like a gazelle caught in a lion's jaws, then went very still, her mouth opening helplessly beneath his, her hands moving to his strong neck as she kissed him deeply, letting her eyes close and her mind fall back into oblivion.

She'd never felt anything like it. Her blood was singing, her body shaking as he slowly pushed her backwards on the couch, and as he lay full-length on it he gently but firmly lifted her slender legs on to it to lie beside him so that their bodies could touch.

Her body seemed magnetised, compelled by some irresistible force of nature to press against his, press against him and feel him, both of them shifting with increasing desire, their mouths hungrily eating each other, tasting, touching, sliding blindly together.

It was a fierce, erotic darkness which consumed them both. His long hands were moving over her. He was breathing so fiercely, his heart banging so violently in his chest, that she could not pretend he didn't feel as overwhelmed by this as she did, and the knowledge of his unreasoning desire made her so excited that she thought she'd lose consciousness.

'Yes...yes...!' he kept muttering in a deep, drugged voice. The hardness of his body was burning, jutting against her stomach through his black trousers and her black silk pyjama jacket.

He shifted his body, and as their sexes pressed together they went completely over the edge. He growled against her mouth, kissed her deeply, let his hands move, one sliding over her breast, the other cupping her rear, making her cry out in agonised excitement, her legs sliding apart so naturally that she had a sudden intolerable, insane need to tear his clothes off, touch him, feel him touch her, give release and find it herself.

'Stop it, stop...' She fought her way free, but she felt drugged by the power of desire, emotion, excitement.

'I don't want to. I feel totally out of control for the first time in my life, and I'm appalled by how much I like it.'

'I don't care how you feel! I hate it and I want it to stop!'

He raised his head. He was darkly flushed, eyes glittering like *Starry Night*, midnight-blue with swirls of light and colour flashing in the violent passion of Van Gogh's visions.

Emma looked into those eyes and felt weak with emotion.

'You can want it to stop,' he said deeply, 'but you can't make it stop. Neither of us can.'

'That's not true,' she said feverishly. 'I'm an adult in control of my own life and if I don't want to feel something I won't feel it. It's a sexual attraction, nothing more, and——'

'Oh, for God's sake!' He gave an angry laugh, staring down at her with wild eyes. 'Look at you! Look how quickly you lost yourself with me just now! You know perfectly well there's more to this than sex!'

'What, then? You tell me, Mr Expert—what exactly is going on between us?'

'I really don't have the first idea. I just know that it's exceptional, whatever it is.'

'Whatever it is! Do you know how stupid you sound? All that——'

'Don't you ever call me stupid!' His hand bit into her chin, and the flash of rage in his blue eyes made her catch her breath. 'I may not have all the answers, but at least I have the guts to do something about this! You may not like being confronted with it, but you can hardly deny it's real—not after the way you just kissed me. And don't blush like a schoolgirl. You're an adult, you're experienced. On your own testimony, you're practically an expert at fending off unwanted kisses! You certainly fended young Toby de Courcey off earlier tonight—I saw you slithering out of his embrace.'

'Don't——'

'Yes, that's right. Blush some more! If you can slither away from Toby, you can slither away from me. But you didn't, did you? Quite the reverse, in spite of your fine protestations. So come on, Miss Super-Cool, Miss Never

Gets Involved, Miss Wouldn't Kiss A Man Unless She
Wanted To—you tell me! What precisely made you throw
the rule-book out of the window for me tonight?'

She couldn't speak. Emotions were whirling like a
storm in her mind. She heard the word 'love' in her mind,
but she couldn't accept that—it was insane—so she
pushed it away and, as she did, she stared into his eyes
and felt as though she was looking death in the face and
had no option but to make violent love with him in
protest against it.

It terrified her.

'Get your filthy hands off me!' she heard herself cry
hoarsely, pushing at him like a wildcat, and he instantly
tried to catch and hold her.

They struggled in angry silence, but in the mêlée of
flailing hands, nails, cries of unreasoning emotion she
managed to get free, stumbling off the couch, staggering
away from him, breathing hard, groping for her balance
in the centre of the room.

He got to his feet and came towards her with a face
like thunder.

She backed away. 'Keep away from me, Patrick, or
I'll scream until somebody comes running to this cabin
to make sure I'm all right!'

He stopped, mouth tightening with anger. 'You're
being childish.'

'I'm protecting myself from your unwanted advances!'

'I shan't even bother picking you up on the word
"unwanted"!'

'I'm very glad to hear it.' She was close to tears now,
biting them back bravely, so confused that she no longer
knew what to do or say, knew only one thing: that she
had to make him leave. 'And I meant what I said. I *will*
scream unless you leave immediately. In fact, I'm going
to count to five, so I'd get moving if I were you.'

'Emma——'

'One,' she said, eyes blazing, at him. 'Two.'

'Look, this won't do you any——'

'Three.'

'You'll still need to make love with me, even if I do leave now!'

'Four.'

'Stop counting at me like that!' His nostrils flared with rage. 'We're stuck together for the next fortnight, and this isn't going to go away! It's going to get stronger! It'll make both our lives hell!'

'Five!' She opened her mouth to scream.

'You obstinate female!' he bit out. He strode to the door, wrenched it open, then glanced back at her over one huge shoulder to say, 'Don't you know that problems can only be solved by confronting them?'

The door slammed behind him.

Emma's eyes closed in a wince. She hated him for that last sentence, because of course he was right, but what did that matter, when the stakes were so very high?

Confronting this—whatever it was—meant nothing more or less than making love to a virtual stranger. He must be mad, she thought angrily, to believe for one second that I would ever consider doing that.

Yet he didn't feel like a stranger. He felt like a man she had known all her life. She remembered the sensation when he'd first kissed her, of entering a different dimension, a dimension that existed only between them, a dimension that had been created with every door in the mind opening between them so that he could walk right through and claim her forever.

Emma sank on to the bed, trembling.

I'm going mad, she thought. I've completely lost it.

The clock ticked gently on the bedside table and she glanced at it, to see that it was now twenty-five past three in the morning.

Just exhaustion, then, she told herself with aching relief. I'm tired and emotional, that's why he was able to rattle me, and that's why I'm spinning like a Catherine-wheel thinking mad thoughts about love and different dimensions and doors opening in my mind.

Emma got into bed, put out the light and told herself she would feel very differently in the morning.

CHAPTER FOUR

BUT she didn't.

In fact, Emma woke up from an intense dream about him, and felt as filled with Patrick as the cabin was filled with sunlight. Staring at the sunlit water patterns playing on the wall, she wondered for a second why she had dreamt about Patrick with such intimacy.

Then she remembered last night, and hot colour flooded her face. He had made passionate love to her, she had reciprocated, and they had talked with such honesty that she was frightened.

Although Emma wanted nothing but truth in her life, she had never expected to find it with a man. Especially not a man like Patrick Kinsella—a playboy.

It was much too disturbing to dwell on, but she had to dwell on it, because in a few minutes she would have to go up on deck for breakfast and come face to face with him.

What was she going to *say* to him? Feeling like this, excited and angry and afraid all at the same time, what could she possibly say to him that would not give her away?

And I mustn't give myself away, she thought with fierce determination. He knows too much already. He made that very clear with his final comment about confronting problems in order to solve them. She winced inside at her own cowardice, but this was a problem she did not wish to confront.

The problem was that he was too experienced. He had known the minute sexual attraction reared between them, just as she had. The only difference between their reactions was that he had welcomed it while she had shied away from it in horror. Regardless of all other points, that reaction had carried on right the way down the line. Emma had no doubt that it would continue to do so, and that meant only one thing—she was in danger from him.

Because of the type of man Patrick was, he would not stop pushing until she caved in. And, because of the power of attraction between them, sooner or later... she would cave in.

I'll just have to keep away from him, she realised. There simply is no other solution.

At the end of the day, Patrick was a playboy, he was cynical, and he was a man who was used to living a carefree bachelor existence. Emma might have been happy to admit that she was cynical where romance was concerned, but that didn't mean she was either a playgirl or uninterested in a relationship.

If she let Patrick get the better of her, he would undoubtedly lose interest and walk away, leaving her to nurse the bitterest wounds of her life. How humiliating, after all! To be seduced then dumped by a notorious playboy! Only a stupid, naïve little teenage girl would let that happen to her.

The best way to handle this, she decided, was to convince him that she was no longer attracted to him. For a second, she indulged in a fantasy conversation with him, where she was strong and convincing. But then she remembered that her fantasy Patrick bore no relation to the real Patrick. He wouldn't meekly agree with her every word or be cowed by a cold look from her. No, the real Patrick would grab her by the scruff of the neck and batter her against a wall until she admitted the truth.

'You tell me!' His words from last night rang sting-ingly in her ears. 'What precisely made you throw the rule-book out of the window for me tonight?'

She winced inside at the thought of answering that question. The last man she had ever expected to throw away the rule-book for was a notorious playboy who lived far beyond cynicism.

And she'd let him kiss her, touch her, make love to her...

She winced again, then determined to push the whole thing from her mind by the simple expedient of telling herself she would deal with Patrick by crossing his bridge when she came to it. After all, who knew how con-vincing she could be until she tried?

Emma got up, showered, washed and blow-dried her hair, then steeled herself to face him. Pulling on a peacock-blue sundress, she slid a pair of gold strappy sandals on to her bare feet and ventured outside her cabin, going up on deck with a determination not to be interested in that pest Patrick Kinsella.

The cool Mediterranean breeze blew her hair back from her bare shoulders as she stepped on deck. Music came from the front. She walked towards it, one hand on the steel railing, and saw a number of orange-yellow sun-loungers, chairs, tables, parasols, all set out on the hot wood, the sun blazing directly down on them, while everyone lay around snoozing.

'Morning!' Liz saw her and waved, then turned the volume down on the radio she was listening to.

'Hi!' Emma waved back. 'Have I missed breakfast?'

''Fraid so.' Liz pushed her yellow baseball cap back on her head. 'But I'm sure they'll rustle up a snack for you, if you're peckish.'

'I'm not really hungry. But I'd love some coffee.' She reached the table beside which Liz lay in a lounger. 'Is it still hot?'

'Sure—help yourself.'

Emma did so, smiling and waving to Toby, Charles and Natasha, who lay near by, all listening to Walkmans.

Her eyes were darting around like mad for a sign of Patrick.

Not that she cared where Patrick was.

She just wondered, that was all.

'Patrick's working,' said Liz, reading her thoughts.

Emma went scarlet, snapping, 'Did I ask where he was?'

Liz frowned, studying her curiously.

Emma's blush deepened. Too late she realised that Liz had been making a casual remark, and not reading her thoughts. She winced inside, took her coffee and sat clumsily down beside Liz.

'So,' she said, trying to cover her stupidity, 'what time do we dock at Málaga?'

'No idea. You'll have to ask Patrick. He's the very important captain.'

'Someone taking my name in vain?' drawled a dark, unforgettable voice from above.

Emma's heart kicked like a startled horse as she forced herself not to stare at the upper deck, her heart banging like mad as Patrick Kinsella descended the steel staircase, looking utterly devastating in black trousers and nothing else.

Of course, she could see him out of the corner of her eye.

He was even more gorgeous than she'd remembered and she felt images explode in her mind of his kiss, how fabulous it had been, how much she had enjoyed every second of it.

She wanted to die.

'Yes, we were, Patrick!' Liz called cheerily, oblivious of Emma's emotions. 'Emma wanted to know what time we dock at Málaga.'

Emma busied herself in drinking her coffee with shaking hands.

'Around midday.' Patrick strolled lazily to stand in front of her sun-lounger, and sank down on it, making her jump and stare at him. 'Hi there,' he murmured smokily, seductively. 'Did you sleep well?'

She spilt a drop of coffee on the deck, blushing as she put the cup on the table near by, aware that Patrick understood completely why she had been so suddenly clumsy.

He leaned close and murmured in her ear, 'You're very jumpy this morning. Nothing to do with last night, I hope?'

'Why should I be?' She kept her voice as low as possible. 'As far as I'm concerned, nothing of any consequence happened last night.'

'Nothing of any consequence...' He watched her, face angry, nodding.

'Absolutely nothing worth remembering.'

'You'll be sorry you said that!' he told her under his breath and, without another word, stood up. 'As there are only two cars meeting us at Málaga docks,' he said loudly to the others, 'I suggest we discuss the arrangements for who will be in which car. What's everyone doing?'

'Well,' said Natasha, 'I'm shopping in Málaga, with Charles and Liz.'

'I'm going into Málaga for a lazy day,' Toby said. 'What about you, Emma? Why not come out with me? I'm sure you'll have fun...'

'Thank you, but no.' Emma shook her head politely, not wishing to give Toby the wrong idea by spending the day alone with him.

Toby nodded, disappointed. 'Are you sure?'

'Yes. It's very kind of you——' Emma smiled to soften the rejection '—but I'd much rather see some historical sites—that kind of thing.'

'Well, that's settled, then,' Patrick drawled with a hard smile of satisfaction. 'Emma and I will take one car and drive into Granada for the day.'

She caught her breath, staring up at him. 'What?'

'You did say you wanted to see Granada, didn't you?'

'I never said I wanted to see it with you!'

His eyes mocked her. 'I distinctly remember hearing you talk about it last night.'

'It was a chance remark, Mr Kinsella, and I did not make it to you!'

'Mr Kinsella?' Patrick drawled. 'How formal of you! Never mind, we'll be on first-name terms by the time we get back from Granada. Meanwhile I simply must go up to the bridge and discuss sailing time.' Turning on his heel, he strode coolly across the hot wooden deck, going back up the steel stairs while Emma glared after him, gibbering with rage.

Then she found herself being stared at by the others. Her face burned like fire. The last thing she wanted was for them to realise there was anything going on between her and Patrick. There *is* nothing going on between me and Patrick, she thought furiously, and I shall make that abundantly clear to him, once and for all, during this wretched trip to Granada.

Angrily, she lay on her stomach on the sun-lounger, took her Walkman out of her handbag, and tried to blot out the whispers of the others by listening to some music.

Damn him for being so clever! He had known she would refuse an invitation from Toby. He knew she wasn't interested in Toby. He knew because he had seen her slither expertly out of Toby's embrace last night—only to succumb passionately to Patrick's a few hours later.

An hour later her face was still burning with angry embarrassment as she saw Patrick stride back on to the deck, and as her eyes traced his body she remembered that passionate embrace of last night. More than an embrace. He had had her horizontal on both the bed and the couch, touching her breasts and thighs and listening to her moan with pleasure.

How humiliating it was to know that she had given in so easily! And even more humiliating to know that it could so easily happen again! Just look at the way she was lying here in the sun, staring secretively through her lashes at his powerful chest, long legs and big, strong hands, remembering every second of his lovemaking last night...

Her skin burned like fire from head to foot. Excited, ashamed, she shifted in the sun-lounger, pressed her inner thighs unconsciously together, horrified by her thoughts and determined to resist them.

'I say,' Toby said suddenly, 'this is hot stuff, Liz!'

'What is?' Liz murmured as the ship lolled gently.

'Your latest novel,' said Toby. '*Savage Desire!*'

'That sounds a bit risqué!' said Charles, perking up.

'I've just got to the bit where the heroine can't stop thinking about the hero's hard-muscled body and what she wants him to do to her.'

Emma went scarlet, tensing, prickling from head to foot. Her eyes shot back again to Patrick, who was standing on the other side of the deck, watching her with a lazy, knowing smile.

'Of course,' said Toby, lying on his stomach on a sun-lounger, 'she hates him passionately, and is madly fighting her desire, but I have high hopes for the next chapter!'

Emma got up, unable to stand the conversation any longer, and walked with tense awareness of Patrick to the drinks table to pour herself some lemon barley water with ice. Her hands trembled and the glass clinked as she poured. Her skin was hot, sun-flushed. Sweat sheened her limbs. She wanted Patrick and hated herself for it.

Patrick watched her, and she trembled more, hating him, loathing him, wanting to kill him because he *knew* how deeply affected she was by him.

'Why do the heroines always hate the heroes?' asked Toby.

'Simple,' said Liz. 'Because the heroines fight the sexual attraction, and——'

Emma banged her glass down on the table with an angry crash. 'Land ahoy!'

Everyone turned to stare at the Spanish city, a heat-haze dancing above the distant white buildings while the Med glittered yellow-blue in the hot sunlight.

'Looking forward to our afternoon and evening in Granada, Miss Baccarat?' drawled Patrick, still watching her flushed, aroused face.

'Not particularly.' Emma summoned an acid smile. 'But I'll go and get changed and try to put a brave face on it!'

Turning, she stamped down to her cabin, angrily aware that part of her fury was directly attributable to her extreme state of sexual arousal. It wasn't fair. Why couldn't she stop feeling so attracted to him? She'd always been able to stop feeling sexually attracted to any man who passed her by. She'd even been able to prevent herself from feeling frustrated by her self-imposed celibacy. So why was she helpless now?

What *was* it about Patrick Kinsella that overpowered her?

Well, he's not overpowering me again, she thought, and cleverly selected jeans and a white top for her day with him. Jeans weren't much of a barrier, but they were a lot better than a skimpy dress.

Oh, but he's probably very practised in the art of taking a girl's jeans off, she thought savagely. After all, he's had plenty of experience. He could probably undo a bra with his teeth. Damned playboys! God, how she hated, loathed, despised him!

The engines stopped suddenly.

Emma went to the windows and looked out to see the crumbling, dirty stone walls of the dock. They had arrived. She would have to go up and face the music—an entire day alone with Patrick.

Taking a deep breath, she picked up her handbag, sunglasses and camera, then went up on deck.

The ship was deserted. Patrick waited alone at the gangplank for her. He wore black trousers and a black polo shirt. His body was superb. His black hair flickered back from his tanned forehead. Dark glasses shielded his eyes. She wanted him so much she could barely stand.

'Hi.' He turned, cool and self-assured.

'Hi.' She stopped in front of him, expressionless.

There was a brief and electrically charged silence. Emma felt that deep intimacy between them, and wondered suddenly if sexual attraction really was all they had. If it was just sex, why did they have this depth of silent communication?

'Shall we go?' Patrick's voice was cool, but she noticed he was no longer mocking or provoking her, and she wondered with a sudden shock if he was as tense as she was. 'The car's waiting just down there...'

They both descended the gangplank. Their bodies were taut with awareness of each other. She walked beside him, shot a brief glance at his profile, and wondered why he should suddenly be tense too.

The car was a white saloon. Getting into it with him created a minefield of awareness because they were shut up together with no escape. The stifling heat made it worse. She was grateful when he switched on the engine and air-conditioning blasted out coldly on to her hot, flushed face.

'We should be in Granada in a couple of hours.' Patrick steered the car away from the docks.

'That will be nice.' All she could think about was him stopping the car and leaning over to kiss her.

The streets of Málaga flashed past, high-rise white skyscrapers reaching to the hot blue sky, palm trees lining the centre of the main road while sexy Spanish señoritas swayed along, causing mayhem among groups of young men on motorbikes.

They slowed at a set of lights and sat there in uncomfortable silence.

'Guess what I'd like to do?' Patrick said suddenly.

'I don't know—what?' she asked stiltedly.

'Stop the car and kiss you senseless.'

'How predictable!' She gave an unsteady laugh and felt her palms begin to sweat. Of course, she would die rather than admit that that was what she'd like too. 'Well, I wouldn't try it if I were you.'

'Did I say I was going to try it?'

'Of course you're going to try it! Don't patronise me— I know what's going on in your head!' Her eyes flashed. 'You're going to take me to Granada, try to wear my resistance down, then pounce on me on the way home tonight!'

He laughed under his breath. 'You really are clever, aren't you?' The car was pulling away in the stream of glittering traffic, palm trees rising like thin green towers in the centre of the road. 'But not quite clever enough. After all, why should I wait all that time when I've got you to myself all day?'

'Because you'd rather I didn't fight,' she said pertly. 'You stopped every time I fought you last night. It clearly doesn't turn you on to have to force your conquests to make love.'

A smile touched the cynical mouth. 'That's what I like about you, Emma. You've got your head screwed on.'

'Yes, and you're not going to screw it off.'

He caught his breath, stared at her, hard mouth parted in an astonished smile. 'Did you just say what I think you said?'

With a brief laugh, she looked away, colouring, and drawled, 'You've got a filthy mind, Mr Kinsella. I just meant that I wouldn't let you overpower my very capable brain with an onslaught of sexual temptation.'

'I'm glad to know I can tempt you.'

'The devil can tempt me too.'

'Yes, but he wouldn't be as honest with you as I am,' Patrick said deeply, and she turned her dark head to look at him in silence, thinking of the honesty he had shown her so far, and knowing he would continue to show it.

They were leaving the city behind now, driving up into the rugged hills of Spain, and the beauty of the desolate, sun-baked earth struck at Emma's heart.

'Are you saying——' she cleared her throat as they drove across that bleached wilderness '—that you really are being completely honest, and always will be?'

He inclined his head, face serious. 'In so far as I can be.'

'Would you agree, then, that your interest in me is completely sexual? And that if you ever conquer me you'll just walk away?'

'No, of course I wouldn't agree with that!' A frown pulled his dark brows together as he glanced at her before glancing back at the deserted road. 'I told you last night that I felt more for you than sexual attraction.'

'But you won't tell me what else you feel.'

'I don't know what else I feel. I've only just met you. Besides, you won't tell me either. Remember? I asked you point-blank why you'd thrown your famous rule-book out of the window, and you became hysterical.'

Her face burned. 'I did not become hysterical.'

'Oh? Then who was that, screaming her head off, slapping and scratching like a wildcat, demanding I leave immediately?' He laughed under his breath as she stared mutinously ahead, her face burning hotter. 'Blushing, too. Do you always blush this much?'

'Only when you're around,' she snapped, then wished she could bite her tongue off.

He laughed softly, slid a hand over her jean-clad thigh. As though stung by a wasp, her thigh jerked away at the same moment as her hand angrily slapped his.

'Don't you touch me!'

His hand slid back on to the steering-wheel and he drawled, 'You want me to touch you, Emma. That's what this is all about.'

The car began to slow. Her eyes began to dart around but there was nothing in sight, just endless sun-bleached earth, the only landmark for miles a sixty-foot-high red metal *torro* celebrating bullfighting.

'Why are we stopping?' she asked tensely.

'So I can remind you that you want me to touch you.'

Her heart started pounding like a drum. 'No! I won't let you——'

'We'll see about that!' he murmured, and stopped the car, turning to her. His hard hands had her by the shoulders before she could struggle away from him and open the passenger-seat door.

She struggled valiantly, but he overpowered her without any trouble at all, and as she screamed and slapped at his hard face he was moving on to her in the front seat, pinning her beneath his powerful body, and suddenly his dark glasses were knocked off by her hands as she fought him, leaving her dazed by the sight of those brilliant blue eyes.

They both stilled, staring at each other, and the leap of desire was excruciating. Patrick shifted his body on her with a low, harsh exclamation, and she felt the burning rigidity of his manhood pressing against her, making the pulse between her thighs spasm hotly.

'Don't...!' Her voice descended to blind, husky panic as his head swooped down. 'Please...!'

His hard mouth closed over hers and she moaned out loud, her hands uncurling on his broad shoulders, feeling her eyes close helplessly, her mouth open like passionate fire beneath his.

It was heaven and hell, dangerous ecstasy sweeping over her as he claimed her in a compelling kiss that made her head spin, made her pulses leap like fire, her blood pumping around her body, little moans coming from the back of her throat as he kissed her deeper, deeper, deeper.

One strong hand moved to the side of the seat, pressed a lever, began pushing her back while he shifted his body with a harsh exclamation of increasing desire, and she felt her jean-clad thighs part for him.

'Please...!' she whispered against his hot mouth. 'Don't do this to me... I can't cope, Patrick...'

'Why can't you cope, Emma?' His voice was ragged; he was still kissing her blindly, his eyes closed and his face darkly flushed.

'Because I don't want this to happen!'

'Yes, you do!' He ravaged her throat with his hot mouth, and it was so exquisite that it made her cry out in appalled response. 'Oh, God, listen to you...' he groaned hoarsely, kissing her deeper, his heart banging like crazy as his long, hard fingers moved up to cover her breasts, stroke her fiercely erect nipples and drive her half mad with excitement.

She felt momentarily lost, arching against him, drugged with him, his touch, his taste, the feel of his hands on her breasts, stroking her nipples, making her think terrible, driven thoughts of wild, frenzied, very necessary lovemaking ...

'Admit you want me to touch you!' Patrick whispered thickly, his mouth moving lower, hotter, fingers fumbling with the buttons of her white top, pushing it aside to bare her breast. His hot mouth closed over her nipple, sucking hungrily while she gasped in violent response. 'Say it out loud! Let me hear you say it.'

'I want you to touch me!' she whispered blindly, moaning as his body moved against hers in torturous excitement.

A car roared past noisily.

Emma's eyes flashed open, blinded by the sunlight, seeing suddenly the scene from outside—herself under Patrick in the front seat of a car, her white jean-clad thighs splayed, her breasts bared ...

'Oh, no!' Horror spilled into her mind. She pushed frenziedly at him, hating herself, hating him even more, slapping and scratching as she fought him off.

'It's all right, it's all right.' His voice was surprisingly gentle, though he didn't release her, just held her with long, firm hands. 'I wasn't going to take it all the way. God knows I want to, but even I draw the line at the front seat of a car in broad daylight!'

Emma whispered, shaking from head to foot, staring up into his hot face in panic. 'I may have admitted I want you, but that doesn't mean I'll let you take me. I'm not interested in a relationship based on sex.'

'Emma, this relationship cannot possibly be based on sex.'

'Why not?'

'Because it didn't start with a physical attraction.'

'Then what did it start with?'

He looked at her warily. 'Honesty?'

She heard her voice take on that peculiarly female huskiness again. 'My honesty—or yours?'

'Both.' His eyes seemed to open that dimension again between them as he studied her.

Emma's heart was skipping lovesick beats.

Patrick said deeply, 'I think we have a lot in common. The cynicism, the disbelief in romance, the sense of isolation from everyone around you. And most of all the longing to find someone with whom you can be completely honest.'

Emma breathed jerkily, her eyes and heart uncertain, longing to believe him. 'But you seem to be much more interested in the sexual attraction. Presumably that means you value sexual honesty more highly than emotional honesty.'

'I'm just responding to the attraction. Can't you understand the difference? If I wanted gratuitous casual sex, I could get it just about anywhere. I'd hardly need to resort to this kind of behaviour. It's not much fun for me to get rejected all the time.'

'I don't reject you all the time,' she muttered shamefully.

He smiled, dropped a long, lingering, sexy kiss on her mouth. 'Mmm. I know... That's what makes it all worthwhile...'

'Don't...' She smiled wryly even as she said it, her green eyes teasing him, already responding like a lover as she ran her fingers through his dark, silky hair. 'We're supposed to be talking things through. Not getting into more trouble by kissing.'

'Death by kissing,' he murmured against her mouth. 'Now there's a lovely way to go!'

Emma laughed huskily, but her hands were firm as they pushed at his hard shoulders. 'Yes, very nice, but hardly practical. I need to think about this before I let it get any further than it has. Don't forget, I've been alone and very happy with it for five years.'

'Yes, and I'm sure that's one reason you're so afraid of this.' He studied her with a frown, one long-fingered hand playing with her dark hair. 'Five years without a lover is too long, Emma.'

Her eyes flashed without warning. 'Must you bring everything back to sex?'

'Must you tear everything away from it?' he fired back shrewdly.

She stared at him without an answer to that, knowing there was truth in the question, yet also knowing that it wasn't the most important thing in life, and must not be if one was to find true happiness.

'No reply?' he murmured, arching dark brows.

'Love is more important than sex, Patrick. I'm not saying I believe in romantic love but I *do* believe in friendship.'

'So do I. And just because I want your body it doesn't mean I don't see you as a person in your own right. If we aren't behaving as friends right now it's because you're so damned hostile to me.'

'Oh, that's right! Blame it all on me!'

'Well, who else can I blame? I'm still treating you just as I did when we first met. In fact, I'm actively *forcing* you to talk to me. I'm quite well aware that you'd prefer to avoid me altogether. But that's only because you're afraid of this sexual frazzle that's——'

'I'm not afraid of it!'

'Prove it.'

'Oh—by going to bed with you? Get lost!'

'No, not by going to bed with me, you idiot! By talking to me.'

'What's this if not talking?'

'Arguing.' His mouth was a cool line.

'Well...you keep pushing me into things. Small wonder I keep arguing with you. What am I supposed to do? Meekly agree with everything you say? I thought we'd already agreed I wasn't a pretty little dolly?'

He laughed, blue eyes dancing. 'You'll never be a dolly—you're far too smart! And I like it that way. There are so many dollies around, Emma. You have no idea how boring it is sometimes to be a man, with women going around batting their eyelashes at you, pretending to be stupid, lying about their real feelings, standing around looking vacuous and wearing tight, sexy, dolly-bird clothes.'

'I would have thought women like that would be right up your street.'

'If they were, I wouldn't be interested in you,' he said flatly. 'So stop arguing with me and start talking, properly, as though I'm a friend.'

'I'm sure that's what the wolf says to Little Red Riding Hood.'

'I may be a wolf, but you're certainly not Little Red Riding Hood!'

Her eyes flashed. 'Why should I pretend to be wide-eyed when I'm not?'

'And why should I pretend to be a romantic wimp when I'm not?'

Her lashes flickered. She studied him in an odd silence, agreeing with what he said, yet wondering if he knew quite how dangerous it was for her to trust him.

'Now look,' he drawled sardonically. 'We're arguing again. I've got a good idea. Why don't we call a truce? Just for today. Sex is what bothers you most about me, so I'll promise not to lay a finger on you until—oh, mid-night tonight—if you'll promise to talk to me.'

Emma smiled, eyes narrowing. 'What's the catch?'

He laughed. 'You have to promise to tell me . . . let's see . . . yes, seven key things about yourself before we get back to the ship.'

'What kind of things?' she asked suspiciously.

'Anything. Just make sure they're all personal, all reasonably interesting keys to your character, and all to do with your emotional self. I don't, for instance, want to hear a boring run-down on your favourite nineteenth-century political speech.'

She laughed against her will. 'Fat chance. I don't have one.'

'Neither do I. So there's something else we have in common.'

'Your terms sound fair. I think I can agree to them.'

'In other words, you think you can come up with some easy ways out and not tell me very much at all,' he drawled wryly.

'No. I'm not going to tell you deeply personal secrets, but I will fulfil my side of the bargain, so long as you fulfil yours.'

'Oh, I'll fulfil mine. Until midnight tonight.'

'And what happens after midnight?'

'This...' He bent his dark head to kiss her mouth slowly, hotly, exquisitely, and as she succumbed to the kiss with reluctant pleasure she closed her eyes, ran her fingers shakingly through his dark hair, and wondered if she would really be able to hold him off until the cruise ended, because she *really* wanted him to make long, slow, passionate love to her...

CHAPTER FIVE

THE cool white stone of the Alhambra Palace gleamed in the hot sunlight, Arabic curls decorating the spire-like archways, gold script glittering against blue mosaic, and all around the scent of exotic flowers, the sound of running water, the sing-song call of birds.

Patrick walked tall, dark and desirable beside Emma. His body was really quite remarkable, especially in those black jeans, muscles bulging from the sleeves of his black polo shirt. As for that cool, charming smile of his . . . he made her pulses throb just to look at him, and she hated herself for wanting him to kiss her, especially since they had made that truce.

'Shall we sit for a while among the fountains?' he asked her as they strolled out of a cool, shady palace room into the sunlight of the Lion Courtyard. 'And talk?'

'Talk. Ah, yes . . .'

He laughed under his breath, and led her with a smile to sit on the white wall around the stone lions. Water streamed from their pursed Arabic mouths. The central fountain was a large Moorish basin. All around them, tourists quietly snapped photographs of the colonnades which rose up to Arabic arches. Emma could think of little but being thoroughly kissed by Patrick, right this minute.

'So——' Patrick watched her through those dark glasses '—what are you going to tell me?'

'Let me think . . .' She was smiling, aware of the desire humming steadily between them like an electric current, just waiting to zap up into powerful action at midnight, and burn them both to death. 'Why don't I tell you about my family?'

'Excellent place to start,' he agreed, a lazy smile on his sardonic mouth. 'But it only counts as one thing. Agreed?'

'Agreed.' As she smiled, Emma's pulses leapt like enchanted butterflies. 'Well, I was born into a very rich family, with houses in London, Hampshire and France. I have a brother called Edward, who lives in France, and whom I never see, and we grew up moving between the three homes.'

'Are your parents still alive?'

'No, they're dead. Killed in a car crash five years ago. I go to their graves once a year with my brother.' She gave a wry laugh. 'We get on so badly that it's the only time we ever see each other. We put flowers on the grave, sit and look at the stone, have lunch, then say goodbye to each other for another year.'

'Why don't you get on?' he asked, frowning.

'Well, let's just say that he's horribly snobbish and superior and puts my back up like mad. He thinks he's cleverer than me and more successful just because he lives in France and has lots of French friends.'

Her brother had been such a sweet, loving boy as a child. They'd got on terribly well. But as he'd grown up he'd just turned into this appalling creature who looked down his nose at everyone and thought he was perfect. Emma forgave him his faults, and prayed every year that he would be changed in his attitudes. But he never was, and while he remained as irritatingly superior she really had nothing to say to him.

'Why should he think he's superior,' asked Patrick, 'just because he lives in France? Were your parents French?'

'No, no!' she laughed. 'My father was frightfully British and my mother was Irish.'

'Oh, was she...?' Those blue eyes were watching her with sudden intensity, and she met them, her own eyes wary, knowing he was thinking something she didn't want him to think.

Ireland glimmered between them like a hazy mirage of magic and romance. Emma began to smile, then lowered her lashes, looking away at a group of Spanish schoolchildren who were obediently following their teacher around the fountains and the stone lions. It seemed sometimes to her that it was the last bastion of romantic nonsense for her, but then it was so safe, wasn't it, to romanticise a country, a people, a national history?

Not at all like romanticising men or love or any kind of dangerously unstable feeling. That kind of romance could only hurt, and anyone with any brains steered clear of such rubbish.

'What was she like, then?' Patrick grinned, clearly not about to give up on this particular subject. 'Your Irish mother?'

Emma gave him a contemptuous look, saying, 'Very beautiful and very determined *not* to be Irish. She'd turn in her grave if she heard you calling her an Irish mother.'

His eyes glimmered with sudden wild darkness, that hard mouth parting as he stared at her in silence.

The doors in her mind were wide open, and as she met his gaze she had a sudden deep impression of him walking through, his mind meeting hers in some inexplicable communion which both shocked and frightened her.

Quickly she looked away, frowning.

What was all this about? He had been thinking something just then, and she badly wanted to know what it was. But if she asked, he might think she was as interested in him as he was in her, and she couldn't let that happen—could she?

'What do you mean,' Patrick asked slowly, watching her still with that dark intensity, 'she was determined not to be Irish?'

Emma tried to keep her voice light, prickling against the deep conviction that she was telling him something important.

'Well, just that she abbreviated her very Irish name— Kathleen—to the English Kathy, changed her accent to an English one, and gave all her children English names.'

'Why did she do that?'

Emma looked at the fountains. 'Oh...she had a nasty childhood in Ireland. Poverty, lots of beatings and a drunken father. She wanted to be an English lady, so she just sort of made herself into one.'

There was a brief silence. Then Patrick said coolly, 'That sounds familiar.'

Emma prickled again, afraid to look at him, afraid of what she would see in his eyes, and very much afraid of how she would feel as their minds locked again in dark communion.

'My parents were both Irish, and both trying not to be.' He spoke expressionlessly, as though unaffected by the twin revelation. 'They called me Patrick, then sent me off to an English boarding-school to learn to be an English gentleman. It was a social-climbing thing. My mother's a terrible snob.'

The rush of water from the fountains seemed to be the only thing Emma could concentrate on in her efforts not to look at him, not to meet his eyes, and above all not to romanticise this unexpected connection between them.

Of course, it meant nothing. It was just a coincidence. And any attempt to see it as anything more was not only dangerous but stupid.

'Have you ever been to Ireland?' he asked lightly.

'No.' She didn't look at him.

'Would you like to go?'

'Yes, of course!' Emma laughed to try to keep the atmosphere even lighter between them, make it seem as though she really didn't care about anything at all, nothing moved her, nothing touched her, and nothing about Patrick Kinsella would ever mean anything to her.

'If you really want to visit it, you can, because I have a home there.'

Her heart skipped a beat as she turned to stare straight into his eyes, pulses racing, wondering if he could possibly be hinting at a future for them, together, as a real couple, not just a sexual relationship.

That deep intimacy was between them, and suddenly Emma felt emotion flooding the darkest recesses of her heart, bringing sunlight and love to banish cynicism.

What else could he possibly be saying? They'd just found something very important in common, and he was offering her the chance not only to visit Ireland, that forbidden sanctuary, but to visit it with him, at some point in the future. And if he saw their relationship extending into the future, then he must want more from her than sex.

She felt light-headed, dizzy with emotion, and as she realised that she thought, My God! Don't tell me I'm capable of falling in love after all!

But then Patrick said casually, 'If you remain friendly with my sister, she'll probably drag you over there one of these days.'

It was a slap in the face and she reacted like a hissing cat. 'Who cares?' She got to her feet angrily without warning. 'I'm bored with the subject.'

Furious at herself for being stupidly romantic, Emma stamped across the courtyard with a taut, set face. I might have known he was just being casually polite! she thought angrily. I should have remembered who I was talking to—a cynical playboy with nothing on his mind but sex, suntans and serious money.

Patrick followed her, crossing the courtyard in a few quick strides, while Emma walked sharply away towards the cool, shady colonnades of the palace.

'What the hell is wrong with you all of a sudden?' he demanded as he caught up with her.

'Nothing.' She kept on walking, determined not to turn stupidly female again. She had been thinking like a misty-eyed teenager. Falling in love indeed! And all because she wanted him to make love to her! I'd be better off being an animal, she thought furiously—at least then I wouldn't confuse lust with love out of sheer stupid femaleness!

'Emma, what is wrong with you?'

'I told you.' She felt so stupidly *hurt*. 'Nothing. Go away and leave me alone.' She blamed him, of course, and hated him, which was even more stupidly female, because her feelings were her own responsibility, and here she was, blaming Patrick just because she herself had got whirled up in a momentary daydream.

His hand took her arm in a hard grip, whirled her to face him. 'I want to know what's wrong with you!'

She gave him a furious, obstinate look. 'Nothing!'

'Look at that face!' He was astonished, eyes widening. 'What did I say to make you so angry?'

'Nothing. And kindly take your hand off my arm. People are staring.'

'I'll give them something even better to stare at if you don't answer my question!' His eyes flashed angry blue. 'The terms of this truce are that you talk to me—and talk truthfully. If you break it like this, Emma, I'll break it too. By kissing you, very forcefully, right now!' His hard fingers tightened on her. 'So start talking and make it good!'

Emma breathed erratically, staring around at the tourists watching, listening, smiling with amusement as they pretended to look at the room while all they were interested in was whether or not Patrick would kiss her till her knees gave way.

'All right!' she said in a taut, angry voice. 'I'll tell you, but it had better constitute another one of my secrets or the whole deal is off.'

'Agreed,' he bit out. 'Just get on with it.'

She hesitated, looking at the buttons on his black polo shirt, trying to think of a plausible lie. But Patrick would know instantly if she lied.

He would know...

Her eyes flashed up to his in shock as she realised she was right: he would know if she lied. Those doors between them had been opened by truth and nothing could ever shut them again. She could run, she could hide, and she could avoid him. But she would never be able to lie to him. Not undetected.

'You're trying to think of a good lie to feed me.' He had even read her mind correctly with those piercing blue eyes fixed on her face. 'I wouldn't try it if I were you. I'll break every rule in the book if one single lie escapes those pretty lips of yours!'

Emma held his gaze for a moment, then looked away, heard her voice say, 'I was angry with you because you said I would go to Ireland if I stayed friends with Liz.'

'Why should that make you angry?'

She hesitated, felt her face suffuse with pink colour, couldn't speak.

'Ah...' He was staring down at her intently. 'I think I know.'

'Well, I——'

'You thought I was leading up to inviting you there with me?'

'Yes.' She couldn't look at him. Her face was proud and her skin deep red. She'd never felt so exposed.

Patrick watched her in silence for a long moment, then said expressionlessly, 'I would have invited you if I'd thought you would come. But it seemed fairly clear that you'd reject that kind of invitation from me. So I didn't bother to offer it.'

Emma felt rescued from some terrible humiliation, and as the muscles of her body slowly relaxed her lashes flickered and she felt able to glance at him, careful to keep her face expressionless, very cool.

'There's really no need to explain, Patrick,' she said. 'I'm quite well aware that I'll never see you again after this cruise, and——'

'What makes you think that?'

'Please!' Her face was coolly contemptuous. 'Spare me the empty promises!'

'It's not an empty promise. In fact, it's not a promise at all. I can't give that kind of promise—I barely know you.'

'You know me well enough to keep trying to get me into bed!' Her eyes flashed, then she controlled her emotions, saying coolly, 'But all that aside, I apologise for losing my temper just now, and I suggest we forget it ever happened. It was unreasonable of me.'

He studied her in silence again, then, slowly, a smile touched his cynical mouth, his eyes started to twinkle, and he drawled, 'So civilised, Emma!'

Her face tightened.

'Back to being Miss Super-Cool, hmm?' he mocked softly. 'Miss Never Gets Involved, Miss Never Loses Her Temper, Miss——'

'Well, if you're going to laugh at me——' She tried furiously to pull away from him.

'Hey!' He held her firmly. 'I am not laughing at you. I just want you to quit this cool, proud superwoman stuff. I admire it. I even understand it. But I can't relax and be myself with it, Emma, any more than you can.' The blue eyes watched her intensely. 'Don't destroy the day when it was going so well. Even if you are angry and hurt.'

Stung, she looked fiercely at him and said, 'OK, it's true! I was angry, and hurt, because I thought the day was going so well, and you ruined it! But I admitted that by telling you why I was angry! I wonder if you'd be quite so quick to admit the truth to me?'

He tensed. 'Probably. Try me.'

'All right—I will! Just why are you so cynical?'

'What . . . ?'

'You heard me.' She lifted her dark head high. 'Why are you such a cynic? Especially when it comes to women? What made you that way?'

He studied her warily. 'That's a long story, and it's not part of the truce that I tell it.'

'I might have known you'd back away from telling me anything seriously personal!' She turned on her heel and walked furiously away from him.

'Hey!' He strode after her, caught her wrist, spun her to face him, eyes furious. 'I thought we had a deal? You tell *me* secrets, but all I do is keep my hands off you.'

She looked up into his handsome face, her eyes angry. 'Suddenly it doesn't seem like such a good deal after all!'

'You wouldn't say that,' he drawled with a lazy, charming smile, 'if I took you into a corner and started making love to you.'

Hot colour rushed up her face. She lowered her lashes, heart beating too fast, and couldn't help noticing the tanned skin of his powerful chest where the neck of his black polo shirt ended. God, he was gorgeous. Why was she such a fool, wanting him like this, when she knew what kind of man he was?

'Or is there more to this than meets the eye?' Patrick murmured, studying her shrewdly. 'The conversation we just had revealed a lot of similarities between us. Is that what caused your sudden temper?'

'Don't be absurd!' Her voice was irritatingly husky. She cleared her throat, not looking at him, her dark head bowed.

'Not scared of having something in common with me, then?' he drawled with cool mockery.

'Not in the least!' Her head came up with icy pride. 'I just want to keep everything on a neutral footing between us from now on!'

He laughed under his breath. 'Well, I doubt that we'll ever manage to be truly neutral, Emma. But I'm prepared to give it a go for the next few minutes, just to get your temper out of the way. Shall we see the gardens? That should take our minds off all this...'

Emma felt unable to argue with him about that, because she knew him well enough by now to know that he wasn't going to rewrite the terms of their truce—not for a million pounds in used Swiss francs. So she let him take her arm and walk her through the rest of the palace rooms, their conversation very neutral and impersonal as they went.

Soon they were in the gardens, surrounded by fabulous trees, flowers and more water—cool, calm ornamental ponds with lilies floating on them, white flowers opening up from thick green leaves to the hot, hot sun.

'I like water-lilies,' Patrick said, keeping everything on safe, neutral territory.

'Yes,' Emma followed suit, pleased to be trite, banal and mindless after that little series of shocks. 'I like water-lilies too.'

He gave her a wry look. She smiled, lowered her lashes, laughed softly.

'Now you've got me pussyfooting around too,' drawled Patrick, but something in the tone of his voice made her look up and see a dark, wary look in his blue eyes, as though he too was disconcerted by what was happening between them.

For a second they watched each other in the hot stillness. Then Emma cleared her throat, anxious to remain on neutral territory. 'Water-lilies have always drawn me. They're a symbolic flower—did you know?'

'Yes, they symbolise rebirth.'

She stared with astonishment, and his hard mouth twisted at the expression on her face. 'Don't look so shocked. I don't spend my life seducing pretty women and carving notches on my bedpost, you know. The occasional thought does run through my mind, and I've long been interested in symbolism.'

'So what do you know about water-lilies and rebirth?'

'I'm very interested in ancient Egypt. I've read the *Book of the Dead* a number of times.'

Her lashes flickered softly. 'I . . . have a copy too.'

Their eyes met piercingly, warily.

Patrick was unsmiling. 'Have you ever been to Egypt?'

'I went there after my parents died.'

'And what prompted that decision?'

Emma looked away at once, and started to walk slowly through the gardens. 'Look—if this is leading to another serious conversation, I want to log it as number three on my secrets list!'

'Fine with me,' he said calmly, falling into step beside her.

'Well, it wasn't just my parents' death that led me to Egypt.' She was horribly aware that this conversation was going even deeper than the previous one. 'It was also that their death coincided with my husband's.'

'Ah...' He walked slowly, eyes watching the hot stone path ahead.

'And I felt,' she said hurriedly, not wishing to dwell on this too much, 'that such a major change had taken place, it warranted a few weeks alone somewhere I could come to terms with it all.'

'What made you choose Egypt?'

She pretended interest in a tree, picking a leaf idly from its fringed branches as she walked past. 'I'd found the *Book of the Dead* in a second-hand shop. It seemed right to go to Egypt itself and sort it all out in my mind.'

'And what conclusions did you come to?'

'My conclusions,' she said coolly, 'will have to be logged as secret number four.'

Patrick was silent for a moment, then nodded slowly and stopped walking, turning to face her, towering over her, his handsome face unsmiling.

Emma took a deep breath and said, 'That I'd had a bad relationship with my father. That it had led to a bad choice of husband. And that their deaths, while tragic, had set me free to begin again.'

'Why was it a bad choice of husband?'

'Because he didn't love me.' She lifted her chin. 'And that's all I'm prepared to tell you.'

To her surprise, he let the subject rest, giving her a brief smile with that hard, sensual, handsome mouth of his, and a second later had started to walk coolly away, saying, 'Shall we do some shopping, then have dinner?'

Emma fell into step beside him and, to her intense relief, they talked about inconsequential things as they left the palace and went out into the busy, winding, medieval streets of the city of Granada.

It was a beautiful afternoon. The city looked stunning bathed in late sunlight, all cobbled streets, bleached buildings, terracotta roofs and ravishing Spanish architecture.

At eight o'clock they had dinner at a restaurant high above the city, perched on a trellised stone balcony, looking out across the countryside, across tall cathedral spires, winding streets, hillside buildings.

'Aren't we being civilised?' Patrick drawled mockingly as he ate his plain grilled fillet steak and drank red wine.

'Marvellously!' she agreed with a glint in her eyes.

'Why, there you are,' he drawled, 'with a knife in your hand, and you clearly have no intention of sticking it in my ribcage!'

'Well, the night is young, darling!'

He laughed, so did she, and the sun began to set over Granada as they ate together lazily, enjoying each other's company, well aware that each had the other's full measure, and happy to relax with that.

Then, as coffee was brought, Patrick said casually, 'Tell me about your husband.'

Tension rose in her as she stared down at her coffee, saying quietly, 'I don't want to tell you about him, Patrick.'

He watched her closely. 'Why not?'

'For the same reasons, I imagine, that you didn't want to tell me what made you so cynical.' She raised her head, met his blue eyes. 'It's a long story, a difficult one, and I don't want to tell it.'

'I'll let it constitute two secrets.' He stirred his coffee lazily.

'No deal.'

'All right, then—three.'

She hesitated, watching him through her lashes.

'You're tempted,' he drawled mockingly, smiling. 'Go on. Three secrets for the price of one.'

Emma considered the proposition.

'While you're thinking about it,' Patrick said coolly, 'you may as well remember that the terms of our truce were very precise. You have to tell me seven secrets. In return for seven secrets, I'll keep my hands off you until midnight. You wouldn't want to break the truce, would you?'

She looked at him through her lashes and they both knew that she would love to be kissed until her head spun into oblivion. They both smiled at each other. She decided it was definitely a good idea to agree to tell him about her husband.

'OK.' She sat back, watching him with a wry smile. 'I accept your proposition. Three secrets for the price of one.'

'Coward!' he drawled softly, watching her with a kissable smile.

She lowered her lashes and blushed, then said, 'I'll try to be brief. My husband was a man called Simon. He was very good-looking. He was twenty when I met him, and an expert in the art of seduction.'

Patrick watched and listened in shrewd silence.

'I believed in romance then,' she said, 'so I was something of a sitting duck. I fell for the whole routine, hook, line and sinker. When he proposed, I felt as though it was a dream come true.' She gave a cynical little laugh, shaking her dark head. 'There he was on one knee wearing a stunning black dinner-jacket, saying, "I love you, my darling, will you marry me?"'

'Very romantic indeed,' Patrick said deeply, and she looked quickly away because she knew he could see the terrible pain and disillusionment that lay behind her recollection of Simon's proposal.

'So I married him.' She laughed again, but her eyes held remembered pain. 'All in white, hundreds of guests, a vast marquee and two hundred crates of champagne. The perfect wedding. We went to Paris for our honeymoon—where else does one go on the perfect honeymoon?'

Patrick smiled with sympathetic cynicism.

'And once the honeymoon was over,' she said coolly, 'he started being unfaithful to me, keeping mistresses, leaving me at home with nothing to do but wait for him to come home with another woman's perfume on his skin.'

'I take it you eventually confronted him?'

'Oh, yes, full of righteous indignation and bewildered pain!' Emma smiled, aware that he did not consider her a fool. 'But of course he was completely unfazed. "You're my wife," he said bluntly, "and I expect you to know your place, turn a blind eye to what I do, and shut up when you're told to."'

Patrick arched cynical brows. 'He sounds very immature.'

'He wanted me to be a showpiece wife, and when I turned out to be a human being he hit me.'

There was a brief, tense silence. Emma did not meet his eyes, just sat there looking out at the red-gold sky streaking across the city spires.

'He hit you?' Patrick asked deeply.

'Once or twice.' She still did not look at him. 'And then he died in a speedboat accident. It was all very sudden. I was twenty-one, we'd only been married two years, and a month later my father died, which left me face to face with *him*.'

'Your parents both died together?'

'Yes, but it was my father I had the biggest problem with. When he died, I realised he'd never loved me, not really, and had just liked boasting to his friends about how pretty and clever and talented his elder daughter was.'

'Expecting you to be perfect...'

'Oh, he really expected that!' She laughed. 'And, of course, I complied. But after his death I found out he wasn't perfect at all. Far from it, in fact. He'd had a secret mistress in the village for twenty years.' She laughed again, shaking her head, remembering her own naïve shock. 'Twenty years. Who would have thought it...?'

'And all that time you thought he was the perfect father?'

'Yes. Even though he used to hit me, and my mother, and my sister, and my brother...' She gave a cool little smile, and said wryly, 'Funny what you'll believe when you're a child, isn't it? I'm so glad I'm not a child any more. Do you know, when people say they wish they were eighteen again I always shudder, because eighteen is the very last age I'd ever want to be again? Not if I had to go through all that again.'

There was a silence. Emma felt self-conscious, sipped her wine with a trembling hand. 'There. Happy now?'

'Yes,' he said deeply, and suddenly his long fingers slid over hers. The tenderness in his eyes made her heart melt. She stared at him in breathless silence for a long time, aware of a certain romanticism filling her stupid, idiotic female heart.

'What can this mean?' Emma asked him huskily. 'You're actually being nice to me for once!'

His lashes flickered against those tough cheekbones. 'Am I?' He unlinked his fingers from hers with a cynical smile. 'Wonders will never cease! Shall we get the bill? It's time we left.'

She tried hard not to feel hurt by his attitude, but could not help knowing that she had invited it with her own flippancy.

It was an uncomfortable drive back to the docks of Málaga.

CHAPTER SIX

THE car slowed at Málaga docks. Patrick presented their documents to the Spanish official, and they were waved through. On the dark waters, the yacht bobbed softly, illuminated by hundreds of tiny lights.

Emma's heart began to beat faster as Patrick switched off the engine and turned to her with a dark, dangerously sexy look in his blue eyes.

'You're not going to break your promise to me, are you?' she asked, trying to sound casually amused when she felt both excited and afraid.

'Of course not,' he said simply.

Her hand fumbled for the door-handle. 'Then in that case you won't mind if I go straight on to the ship?'

'Not at all. I have to deal with the return of this hire car anyway, so I'll see you in the morning.'

'OK.' She opened the door.

His hand caught her wrist, made her heart leap as he drawled, 'But I feel we've made some serious progress today, Emma, and I'd like to remind you of the sacrifice I made in order to get that progress made.'

'It was a sacrifice, was it?' she said huskily, smiling, her pulses leaping at his touch.

'Spending a whole day in your company without kissing or touching you? Yes, it was a huge sacrifice.'

'You did rather more than kiss and touch me on the drive to Granada.'

He laughed under his breath. 'Nobody's perfect. And I did keep my promise to you. I still am. It's only eleven o'clock, and you have no idea how very much I'd like to make love to you right now.'

'But you're not going to,' she said unsteadily, staring at his hard mouth. 'Are you? Because it would be reneging on a deal.'

'Precisely.' His long fingers stroked her wrist as he watched her. 'I hope that makes you trust me a little more.'

'It's never a good idea to trust a wolf...'

'I'm a wolf, am I?' he drawled, smiling. 'And you're some kind of saint, I suppose?'

'I'm not a saint, but I'm not promiscuous either.'

'Neither am I.'

'Your reputation says otherwise.'

'I'm myself, Emma. Not my reputation.' His blue eyes were hard. 'I'm also thirty-seven years old. Hardly the kind of age group where men leap from bed to bed without serious dissatisfaction. It's not my idea of heaven to make love to a woman I don't respect. Sexy, but not enjoyable. Leaves a very nasty taste.'

'Well, you're the expert.'

'Hey...' His long fingers were still caressing her wrist. 'It's your mind I'm interested in, Emma. Even if it does come attached to a stunningly sexy body.'

She laughed. 'Are you trying to tell me you only want to make love to my mind?'

'That's precisely what I'm telling you.'

She studied his clever face and wanted to melt inside, because it was something she had always wanted a man she respected to say to her. But melting inside was dangerous with a man like Patrick Kinsella. Her instincts told her he was wonderful, but logic told her he was an absolute bastard.

'Of course,' he murmured, 'I'm delighted to say I'll be making love to your mind via your very delectable body.'

'You talk as though it's a certainty that I'll let you touch me.'

'I think it's almost a hundred per cent certain.'

Emma's smile froze. 'Keep dreaming,' she drawled, fumbling for the door-handle. 'It'll never happen.' She opened the door, sliding out, pulses fluttering as his long fingers released her wrist. 'I'll see you in the morning, Patrick...'

She was trembling inside as she walked unsteadily to the yacht. This whole thing was moving much too fast for her. She was now getting to the stage where she had to pretend cynicism in an effort to stop herself liking, trusting, wanting him.

The yacht was silent, deserted. Emma went straight down to her cabin. It was warm, silent, dimly lit, but nothing could soothe her disturbed peace of mind.

Everything that had happened between them today had been good. Even their arguments had been both satisfying and filled with blazing honesty. As for that mind-bendingly exquisite kiss on the way to Granada...

She sighed, getting undressed, then sliding into the bed. If she didn't believe in his honesty, she wouldn't be so confused, so attracted. He would be just another playboy chancing his arm, trying to get her into bed, pulling out all the stops.

But she *did* believe he told the truth. And frequently at great risk to his cause.

After all, if he did just want to get her into bed, surely he would fare better by declaring undying love, showering her with false compliments and pretending to be besotted with her rather than sexually overwhelmed?

Not that any of that would turn her head. And she had made that clear from the beginning. So perhaps he was just plain clever enough to realise that flattery and sweet nothings wouldn't work on her, but that honesty would.

Turning over in bed, she switched off the light.

The truth was that she would do anything rather than completely trust and believe in Patrick. Even though all her instincts told her he was truthful. Even though his every word and deed told her he was truthful.

Was she scared? Was that it? Was she scared to trust him in case she actually began to feel too much for him?

It had been five years since Simon died. Those years had been spent carefully peeling away the layers of artifice and pretence. Rejecting the sickening hypocrisy of society. Giving away all her expensive, glittery clothes. Getting rid of the perfect people, the perfect home, the perfect car, the perfect lifestyle...

Truth was what she had demanded, both in the right to express her own feelings and the right to see the world as it was.

Now along had come a man who felt as she did, thought as she did. It would be so much easier if she could just tell herself that Patrick had cleverly noted down her attitudes and then, calculatingly, mirrored them in order to seduce her.

But that wasn't the truth. They had had two very frank conversations when they'd first met, and those conversations had led directly to their powerful attraction to each other.

He might have the reputation of a playboy, but he had the mind of a king—just, intelligent, wise, kind, sensitive, powerful... All right, he was a cynic in many ways, but what was that old phrase?

'There's nothing more cynical than a disillusioned romantic,' she recalled, aloud.

Emma stared at the dark ceiling and realised she could just as easily have been describing herself as Patrick. She was a disillusioned romantic, too. All those dreams of love when she was a little girl had ended in nightmarish disillusion when she'd first discovered that her husband was an adulterer who did not love her, and then discovered that her father had been an adulterer who had not truly loved his wife.

Two men, both holding her romantic dreams in their hands, who had crushed them with cold indifference, leaving her to believe in nothing but herself.

Had that happened to Patrick too? She couldn't believe that it had. He couldn't have been that romantic as a young man, or why would he have gained the reputation he had? And if he had spent his young adult life seducing every woman in sight, how could he have had any romantic illusions shattered?

It was an insoluble problem. She wished suddenly that she had asked Patrick more questions about himself. All she knew about his background was that he felt romantic about Ireland due to his parents trying to make him English when he wasn't—at least, not by birth.

That was another weird thing. They had a number of things in common, but the link to Ireland was kind of spooky. It was spooky enough that they should both feel romantic about the country, but even more spooky that their parents had tried to cut themselves off from their Irish roots.

She wondered, as she began to fall asleep, if there were any other weird things they might have in common...

Repeated knocking on her door woke her at nine o'clock the next morning. Emma blinked sleepily, heard the knocking again, and jumped out of bed, her heart hammering.

Patrick!

Who else could it be? She checked that her pyjamas looked decent, then padded barefoot to the door, her pulses racing like wildfire as she opened it and felt her heart sink with disappointment.

'Morning!' Toby stood before her in jeans and a blue jumper.

She stared at him in confusion and disappointment.

'Just thought I'd come and warn you that breakfast is fast disappearing upstairs! Aren't you hungry?'

'Not really.' Emma ran a sleepy hand through her hair. 'But I could do with some coffee and orange juice.'

'Well, hurry up and get dressed then, sweetie. Here——' He walked into the cabin, closed the door, and began looking through her wardrobe. 'I'll pick out some clothes for you while you jump in the shower.'

Emma stared at him incredulously. 'Just a minute! I don't——'

'Hurry up!' Toby giggled, amused by her shocked expression.

'Toby, much as I appreciate your concern, I really must ask you——'

'Don't be silly!' Toby hustled her towards the bathroom. 'I'm not going to jump on you or bash the bathroom door down! But I told the stewards not to clear everything away until I came back. Come on, come on—I'm starving to death because of you!'

Emma hesitated, then went into the bathroom, locked and bolted the door, and started sleepily pulling her pyjamas off before stumbling into the shower.

Toby was a harmless sort of boy. He was hardly going to try and seduce her, and even if he did she felt sure she could cope with him.

Her shower was brief, and woke her up. When she emerged dripping wet, she chose a big towelling robe to wrap herself in, just in case harmless little Toby *did* happen to try anything funny.

Going back into her cabin, she was irritated to find Toby lounging on the bed.

There was a loud knock at the door.

'That'll be Liz,' Toby said, still lounging on her bed. 'She wants to get some work done with you this morning before we reach Tangier.'

Emma gritted her teeth. 'What is this—Grand Central Station or my private cabin?'

Walking to the door, she opened it expecting to see Liz. Her heart stopped beating when she saw who it really was.

'Good morning,' drawled Patrick, towering in the doorway, blue eyes filled with charm and sex appeal as he let them move slowly to the wet skin at the neck of her towelling robe. 'You're even more beautiful in the——'

'Hi, Patrick!' Toby called cheerfully from the bed.

Patrick's eyes shot to stare at the younger man in horror, and Emma felt sick as she watched the colour drain from his face, the charm dissolve into shock, and then, within seconds, into cold fury.

'I...' Emma's voice shook. 'I was just asking Toby to leave when you knocked and——'

'Sure!' Patrick turned on his heel and strode away without another word.

'Has he gone?' Toby slid off the bed and trotted over to the open door. 'Wonder why he stormed off like that?'

Trembling, Emma turned to face him and realised the extent of the damage he had done. 'Look, Toby, would you please just leave?'

He studied her closely. 'I haven't stumbled on to an existing fling, have I, Emma? Was Patrick jealous? Does he think you're his property?'

'No!' she denied hotly. 'There's nothing whatever between myself and Patrick!'

'But you did spend the day together yesterday...'

'Because we both wanted to go to Granada—that's all!' Emma was still flustered and trembling after Patrick's display of anger, and she needed to be alone to think about how to deal with it. 'Look, Toby, would you just go, please? I'd like to get dressed in private.'

'OK.' He smiled, moved into the doorway. 'So long as we can spend the day together. Just you and I.'

Emma was desperate to get rid of him. 'I'll just see you on deck—OK?'

Closing the door, she leant on it, breathing unsteadily. Patrick would think she was a cheap little... Well, it didn't bear thinking about. She winced at how the scene must have looked to him, with her naked beneath a bathrobe and Toby lying on her bed.

Suddenly she realised that what Patrick Kinsella thought about her mattered. It mattered very much.

I have to see him, she thought frantically, to explain. It occurred to her that the incident had given her the perfect opportunity to get rid of Patrick once and for all, but that was not the overriding thought in her mind— the overriding thought was to make him see her again as he had seen her last night, all yesterday, and all the day before. Untainted by a casual attitude towards sex, men and relationships.

Of course she wanted Patrick to stop pursuing her. Of course she wanted him to leave her alone. It was just that she couldn't allow him to think of her as cheap. That was all.

At any rate, she was dressed now, zipping up her blue jeans with shaking hands and thrusting her feet into flat gold sandals, her damp dark hair falling straight and clean around her pale, anxious face, leaving wet marks on the red top she wore.

Running without thought to the door, she was out in the corridor and up the stairs, breathless, her green eyes darting around for Patrick.

The sunlit deck was filled with music, laughter and talking. Emma stared up at the seating area, saw everyone there but Patrick. Then she looked in the other direction and saw him.

He stood alone at the far end of the yacht, leaning on the railings, staring broodingly out at the glittering blue sea, the wind blowing his black hair back from his hard, handsome face.

Taking a deep breath, Emma approached him with as much brave trepidation as one would approach an angry lion.

'Hi.' Her voice was unsure as she reached him, stood watching him.

Patrick turned his dark head to stare contemptuously down at her from his incredible height of six feet six, and made her feel about two inches tall herself.

'Look…Patrick…I realise the way it must have looked downstairs, but——'

'What you do in your private life,' he said icily, 'is none of my business.'

'I'm aware of that!'

'Then go away.' He shrugged broad shoulders, face tough. 'And carry on with what you were doing.'

Emma took a long breath. 'Look … Toby came to my door and said breakfast was waiting for me up here. He sort of hustled me into the shower—and don't laugh at me, Patrick! I'm telling you the truth!'

'Don't bother, darling. I saw the truth with my own eyes, and it was more than obvious what was going on.'

'You don't seriously believe I'd have a gratuitous piece of early morning sex with Toby de Courcey, do you?' Her green eyes blazed with righteous indignation. 'If you do, it's only because it's the kind of thing you've been trying to get from me since I boarded this ship!'

'Didn't give it to me, though, did you?' His voice was harsh with temper and contempt. 'What's he got that I haven't? Oh, no, don't tell me; let me guess. He's young and foolish and you can wrap him around your little finger.'

'What?' Emma stared at him in stupefaction.

'Well, isn't that the kind of man—boy, I should say—you clearly prefer?'

'No, it is not! I have almost nothing to say to Toby. What's the matter with you?' Her heart beat with anger and hurt that he should disrespect her so much. 'I thought I'd made it very clear that I wasn't interested in any kind of male friendship at the moment. And even if I was interested, it wouldn't be with Toby de Courcey!'

He smiled tightly. 'But he was lying on your bed, quite by chance, and you were wearing nothing whatsoever under your dressing-gown! Are you normally in the habit of taking showers and wandering around naked while men loll about on your bed?'

'Toby's harmless!' she snapped furiously. 'I didn't believe he'd make a serious pass at me.'

He laughed harshly. Her face flushed. She turned to go, her green eyes like black pools of pain and anger. 'Put it like this—I wouldn't risk taking a shower if *you* were anywhere near me!'

She stormed away from him.

'Wait!' He caught her arm, spun her to face him, staring down at her with hellish eyes. 'Why wouldn't you? Take a shower if I was near? Why trust him and not me?'

'Why do you think?' she laughed angrily.

There was a brief silence as he stared at her, eyes narrowed, thinking rapidly. Then he said slowly, 'Because you invited him . . .'

'Look—Toby did not come to my cabin at my invitation! He just turned up out of the blue——'

'Don't we all!' drawled Patrick nastily.

'It wasn't like the way you turned up, Patrick! He didn't try to kiss me, and he certainly wouldn't have succeeded if he had——'

'Really?' he drawled, blue eyes cynical. 'What made me so different? Oh, I suppose I was more forceful than Toby. Poor boy—he doesn't have my height or physical strength, does he, so it wouldn't be so easy for him to pin you down on the bed and——?'

'He wouldn't even have considered doing it!'

'My God, I almost believe you mean that!' He laughed at her with a flash of contempt in his blue eyes. 'Shame you're such a smooth operator, though, and so very cynical—or should I say clinical?—about men! Nobody as clever as you could possibly be that naïve!'

'He didn't lay a hand on me!'

'He was waiting on the bed for his opportunity, though?'

'I don't know what he was doing on the bed!'

'But you were naked beneath that robe, weren't you?' His voice shook as his hands shot out to grip her shoulders, shaking her as though she were a rag doll. 'Did you take a shower before or after sex? Or were you gearing up to give him a free floor-show before you let him——?'

'How dare you even accuse me of that?' she said fiercely. 'No woman in her right mind would behave like——'

'You'd be surprised what women will do!' he ground out harshly. 'Or do you want the low-down on women I have bedded, and just what they were prepared to do?'

'No, I most certainly do not!'

'Why not? I thought you were a cynic from way back?'

'Not in the way you are! Not sexually!'

'So you keep telling me. And I believed it, too, until I saw Toby lying on your bed—waiting for you to continue initiating him.'

'Why, you——'

'Don't look so shocked—what was I supposed to think? The situation seemed crystal-clear to me!'

'Well, you were wrong about the situation!' Her eyes flared as she pushed him away from her, pain and anger warring in her heart. 'And that's not the only thing you were wrong about! You were wrong to think we had anything in common, wrong to think I wanted you, wrong to think I'd ever give in to a man with a mind like——'

'Look at the situation! What would anyone have thought, let alone a man with reason to be jealous?'

'Jealous?' For a second, she was idiotically touched. Patrick? Jealous? Her heart sang with stupid romantic pleasure. Then she remembered how clever he was, and her eyes flared with anger. 'Oh, that really is a cheap trick, Patrick! Trying to win me over by pretending you were jealous——'

'Why should I pretend?'

'To make me think it was romantic jealousy, Patrick, when it was clearly nothing but sexual! You want to take me to bed, and so you felt jealous when you thought Toby had succeeded where you'd failed! Go on—find a way to deny the truth of that particular statement!'

'I wouldn't waste my time.'

'Good! And I'm not going to waste anymore of *my* time on *you*!' She turned to storm away, her heart buzzing with pain and angry confusion.

'Hey!' He caught her arm, whirled her to face him, the sun blazing down over them both as the yacht sailed along through those glittering blue waters. 'Don't walk out like that.'

'I really don't think there's anything more to be said.' Her eyes flared hurt, angry green.

'Because we're arguing? Don't be so childish! Arguing is part of a relationship.'

'We don't have a relationship, Patrick.'

'Don't lie! We became involved the minute our eyes met!'

Her breath caught at the truth of that statement, and she couldn't speak for a second, just stared at him, half of her longing to believe him, while the other half fought against the danger, the terrible danger, of letting her heart rule her head.

'Don't you know it even yet?' His voice was deep and his eyes wild as he bent his dark head close to her, his mouth almost touching hers. 'Or do I have to spell everything out to you, step by step?'

Her heart beat like a crazy hammer. 'What are you saying, Patrick? That there's more to this than just a physical attraction?'

'Well, if there isn't, Emma, why did you feel the need to come and explain yourself to me?'

Emma felt breathless, staring into his tough, clever face, and found herself unable to answer, afraid to answer because she knew her voice would be shaky, and she couldn't bear to see the loss of respect in his eyes when she gave a pathetic excuse.

'What I thought of you,' he said flatly, 'was important enough to you to make you come and see me privately. Doesn't that tell you how involved you already are with me?'

It was difficult to breathe. 'I just didn't want you to think I was having a gratuitous affair with Toby.'

'Surely it was the perfect way to stop me chasing you?'

'Yes, but . . . but I didn't want you to think I was that kind of woman.'

'So you care what I think of you?'

'Only to a certain degree.'

Patrick laughed angrily. 'And what, precisely, does that mean?'

'That I want you to stop chasing me, but I don't want it to be because you think I'm cheap.'

'In other words you want to retain my respect for you?' He arched dark brows. 'While telling me to get lost?'

'Yes.' She flushed hotly.

'But you don't care a damn about me?' His mouth was a hard, angry line. 'I mean nothing to you?'

'Well—do I mean anything to you?' she asked huskily, uncertainly.

He studied her in silence for a moment, then said tersely, 'You did. But if you're serious in what you're saying, if you really don't give a damn about me, then why should I continue to feel anything for you?'

'Because...' She stared at him as the word trailed off into nothingness, then heard herself ask plaintively, 'Patrick—what do I mean to you?'

He hesitated, then looked away. 'I don't know. But it's more than a physical attraction.'

Emma's heart beat crazily. She felt as though she was spinning into eternity, like a singing Catherine-wheel blazing in all the golden colours of romance.

'So...' Patrick watched her coolly '...you don't reciprocate?'

Terror ended her flight of romantic fantasy—terror of getting hurt, of being a fool, of ending up the latest broken heart in his long list of seduced women.

What could she say to him but 'I'm...I'm not sure'?

There was a long, tense silence while he watched her with narrowed eyes, his mouth a hard line, and his long fingers biting into her wrist.

'Fine,' he drawled sardonically. 'Then let's just leave it at that, shall we? I shan't bother to chase a reluctant prey any more.'

Emma felt nailed through the heart as Patrick released her, strode coolly away down the deck without another word, and left her to stare after him with an overpowering sense of loss.

She wanted to run after him and tell him to come back. But she didn't move. She was so immobile that she almost wondered if her feet were nailed to the floor. Inside, the emotions were tearing at her like savage dogs fighting for supremacy.

Respect, desire and love warred against pride, pain and fear.

If Patrick were anyone but Patrick, she would undoubtedly have gone after him, smiled at him, told him she liked him very much and wanted to retain his friendship.

But because he was Patrick she did nothing.

It was fear, more than anything, that stopped her. She was so afraid of getting hurt, and although Patrick's reputation had a lot to do with that fear she was beginning to realise that there was rather more to it than that.

Plenty of other people had reputations as playboys. She had never been this afraid of them—or, rather, of letting herself be vulnerable with them.

So what did that mean? She winced inside. She didn't want to accept what that meant. She didn't want to realise quite how vulnerable she really was to Patrick Kinsella.

Turning, she gripped the railings of the yacht with trembling hands, staring fixedly out at the sea and the gulls that swooped to play with the white-capped wake.

You should be pleased, she told herself. Patrick's going to leave you alone from now on. But of course she wasn't pleased. In fact, she felt like curling up on the hot deck and crying her eyes out.

'There you are!' Liz called brightly behind her.

Emma blinked the hot tears back before turning to face her, struggling to look unemotional. 'Hi! Just taking a breath of fresh air before coming to join you for breakfast.'

'There's not much food left——'

'I only wanted coffee.' Emma walked to join her with a brittle smile. 'What time do we dock at Tangier this afternoon?'

'Two,' said Liz as they both walked back up to the other end of the yacht in the hot sunshine. 'I thought we could get some work done before then, though. Would you mind...?'

'Not at all,' said Emma. It will take my mind off my heart, she added silently.

They took a fresh pot of coffee to Patrick's study on the top deck, and Emma sat down behind the mahogany desk, seeing his presence everywhere: in the dark masculine colours of the room, the rows of intellectual books on the shelves, and the passionate intensity of the wild, vibrantly coloured paintings on the walls. It reaffirmed her respect for him, and her deep understanding of his nature. She was afraid all over again, almost feeling wary just looking at this, his room.

Liz reclined on the couch and dictated while Emma scribbled everything down in shorthand.

If Emma had hoped to take her mind off Patrick, she was horribly mistaken. The book Liz was in the middle of writing suddenly seemed more than just the usual romance: every damned sentence echoed the way Emma was feeling about Patrick.

'...Susannah couldn't believe this was happening,' Liz was saying at midday. 'To find herself falling in love with a man like this—a cynical playboy who had broken hearts all over the world...'

Emma scribbled, feeling sick with fear.

'Yet he seemed so sincere. Susannah believed he had been telling the truth when he'd said he felt more for her than just physical attraction——'

Emma ran a shaky hand over her eyes, thinking, I can't stand this.

'What's wrong?' Liz finally noticed her distress and sat up, staring at her with concern.

'Nothing.' Emma tried to pull herself together. 'Carry on...'

Liz frowned. 'You've been restless and edgy all morning. There must be something wrong. I am your friend, you know...can't you tell me?'

'I...' She hesitated, then shook her head. 'No, it's nothing.'

There was a brief silence. Liz watched her, then said, 'Sometimes I feel amazed at the way life imitates art—don't you?'

Emma met her eyes with dark anguish.

'You know,' Liz said casually, 'it's so nice for me to see Patrick again. We so rarely meet up. He's got such a busy life, so have I, and I'm pleasantly surprised to see how much he's changed in the last two years.'

'Look, Liz, I don't want to——'

'He's had such a tough life,' Liz cut across her husky words. 'I'm glad he's come full circle and completely accepted himself. It was touch and go for a long time after his wife died.'

Emma's jaw dropped and she stared at Liz in stunned silence for a long time, then heard her disbelieving voice ask, '*Wife*? Did you say his *wife*?'

'Oh, didn't you know?'

'And she *died*? You said his wife *died*?' Just saying it made Emma's mind reel. The string of coincidences clattered deeper into place like a line of falling dominoes, from the first moment she had met his eyes and seen his brutal, truthful mind to this moment now, when she sat listening to his sister talk about his deceased wife.

'Yes, Patrick was married at a very young age. One of those awful perfect marriages, where both parties are just trying to live an illusion, and end up getting totally smashed to bits by it in the end. Patrick suffered as much as she did, of course, and nearly went mad with grief when she died.'

Emma couldn't speak. She was afraid to reveal to Liz how emotionally affected she was by this series of revelations. It took every ounce of self-control to keep her face calm, while inside fighting the rise of love, excitement, desire, fear...

'He'd tried so hard,' said Liz, 'to live up to our parents' expectations. The perfect exam results, head boy at school, a perfect degree—with honours and distinction—and then the perfect wife combined with the perfect career.'

'How...?' Emma struggled to think, to speak, her voice shaking. 'How old was he when she died?'

'Twenty-eight,' said Liz. 'He's thirty-seven now, so it was almost ten years ago—but what a spectacular ten years! It was as though he'd been locked up like a tiger in a cage all his life, and as soon as Annabel died he really kicked his way out of that cage! Roaring and snarling, off on the rampage, seducing every woman in sight, drinking far too much whisky and getting himself into all sorts of trouble.'

'All the stories are true, then?' Emma asked. 'About his wild reputation?'

Liz studied her with clear eyes. 'Yes, but you mustn't judge him on that basis, Emma. You have to look at the whole picture. You see, he needed to do it. It was the only way for him to destroy the strait-jacket of perfection. How else but to rip it to shreds with as much imperfect behaviour as——?'

The telephone on the desk rang. Emma snatched it up. 'Hello?'

A pause, then, 'I'd like to speak to my sister.'

The hard, hostile voice was Patrick's, and it made her heart leap into the air like a wild bird startled by gunshot.

'Yes, of course.' Her voice was as cold and unfriendly as his. She handed the receiver to Liz. 'Your brother.'

Liz took the phone, and spoke briefly while Emma listened, struggling to appear unaffected, yet she felt hurt by her own pride, her own determination to make Patrick think she didn't care that they had stopped being involved. Why had she used that voice on him? Why hadn't she tried to sound reasonably friendly? Because he wasn't friendly to me, she realised, and I responded in kind rather than reveal my own hurt.

'I'll have to go out on deck.' Liz replaced the receiver and met Emma's eyes. 'He wants to discuss the arrangements for our tour of Tangier. I think we're all going together this time.'

Emma's heart twisted but she smiled very naturally, hurting badly inside as she presented a perfect persona to her friend. 'That'll be fun. I like being a tourist among friends!'

Liz laughed, accepting at once that Emma was being truthful, and left the room.

The minute the door closed, pain seeped like blood into Emma's eyes and she closed them, swallowing hard on the knot of pain in her chest.

After five years of demanding the right to express her true emotions she was suddenly hiding them as skilfully as she had during her childhood. Why?

There seemed only one logical explanation: she was in love.

I can't possibly be in love, she told herself in a fierce, almost defensive way. It's ridiculous to fall in love that quickly. It's nothing short of lunacy.

Oh, really? she thought bleakly. Then why do I feel like this?

CHAPTER SEVEN

WHEN Emma went up on deck later, she appeared terribly confident, cool and composed. She wore a stylish white sundress, strappy and sexy, her dark hair loose around her bare golden shoulders.

Inside, she was terrified of what was happening, desperately fighting her emotions and struggling to hide them from everyone, but most of all from Patrick himself.

He was the first person she saw.

He stood with the others by the gangplank, his hands thrust into his grey trouser pockets, a white shirt open at the throat, his black hair flickering around his handsome face in the warm breeze. The others stood around him, but they might just as well have been cardboard cut-outs. Life focused on Patrick, every physical response she had focused on him. She felt so much for him that she could barely walk, barely put one foot in front of the other, but she did, stylishly, smiling at Toby rather than ever, ever, *ever* meet Patrick's eyes.

'I hear we're all off sightseeing together.' She went to stand beside Toby. Patrick appeared completely unaffected. He hadn't even glanced at her.

'Yes, isn't it fun?' Toby laughed. 'Patrick's hired a mini-bus. It looks like hell on six wheels. He had to negotiate for twenty minutes with some disreputable-looking character in order to get it.'

'And paid through the back teeth for the privilege,' Patrick drawled with lazy amusement, not even glancing

at Emma. 'But now we're all here, we may as well go
and board the damned thing.'

Emma gave a light laugh, her green eyes dancing with
the sheer holiday fun of it all, while inside her heart was
being clawed to pieces because Patrick didn't care, he
really didn't give a damn that it was all over between
them.

She walked down the gangplank beside Toby, aware
that she was using him as a shield, hating herself for
doing so, yet so appalled by her own pain and vulnerability that she felt desperate for help, any kind of help,
anywhere she could get it.

'Isn't it comical?' Toby giggled, stopping in front of
the mini-bus.

Emma looked up at it indifferently. All she cared about
was keeping her feelings well and truly hidden from
Patrick. It took every ounce of will-power she had.

'It's certainly not a luxury coach!' she said lightly.

'It was the best I could do,' Patrick drawled in a cool,
cynical voice, and strode to the door of the dusty, bat-
tered old vehicle. 'I forgot to book something when we
left Spain.'

'Too busy wining and dining Emma.' Charles threw
Emma a charming smile and nudged her gently. 'Can't
say I blame him, though. She's a real peach!'

'Oy!' Toby put an arm around Emma. 'Hands off,
Charles! She's mine!'

Patrick laughed sardonically, drawling, 'Well, at least
I don't have to be responsible for her again. She can be
an argumentative little witch.'

Emma fought hard to keep her smile pinned to her
face, but inside she was thinking, You bastard, how could
you say that with such blasé cruelty? How could you,
how could you...?

Natasha and Patrick boarded the dusty mini-bus
together. Emma deliberately loitered with Toby and

Charles, careful to let her light laughter echo in the hot afternoon as she flirted blindly, not even noticing the smiles of the two men, thinking only of Patrick sitting aboard the bus with Natasha and hoping he heard her.

When they boarded a few minutes later, Charles sat alone, saying he wanted to concentrate on the tour. Toby took Emma down to the back of the bus and sat with her there.

'Just like being at the pictures!' Toby commented, putting an arm around her and grinning. 'Maybe we could smooch while——'

'I've never been to Tangier before,' Emma cut in with a tight smile. 'I hate to be a bore, but I'd really like to look at the scenery.'

'And not smooch?' He made a sweet little face.

'And not smooch,' she agreed, smiling to soften the rejection. 'I'd also hate to give you the wrong idea, Toby. I may be flirting with you, but that doesn't mean I'm feeling anything other than flirtatious.'

He grinned. 'What's wrong with that? I flirt a lot too. Don't apologise for flirting back with me.'

'OK. Well, let's hope we enjoy the day.'

But she very much doubted that she would. As her head turned from Toby, her eyes automatically sought out Patrick, and she could see him in the front seat, his dark head turned to talk to Natasha, her head leaning close to his as her laughter echoed in silvery flirtation.

The driver started the engine, which spluttered in protest, and they chugged away with a deafening rattle.

Emma tried to stare out of the window, but her eyes kept flicking back to Patrick and Natasha in the front seat. She felt even more clawed, even more hurt. But at least she didn't have to exercise such strenuous self-control to hide her feelings now that Patrick couldn't see her.

He would know, of course, how she was feeling, if she once lifted that iron self-control.

I shouldn't be doing this, she thought angrily, staring
out at the arid scenery. I spent the first twenty-one years
of my life pretending not to have real feelings, and I'm
not doing it again.

But she was doing it. And she would continue to do
it. There was only one imperative planted in her mind
now—preventing Patrick seeing how deeply he affected
her emotions.

What a coward I am, she thought grimly. So much
for truth, self-expression and authenticity.

The bus wheezed up a steep winding hill above the
city. Mosque towers rose up against the blue sky, white
and curly with Arab decoration. Expensive villas lined
the hillsides, overlooking the huddled buildings far below
that led to the bazaars.

'And here on our right,' jabbered the Moroccan guide
into his crackly microphone, 'is the villa where Barbara
Hutton used to live!'

Emma looked blankly at Barbara Hutton's villa. A
poor little rich girl who never found love. Is that how
I'm going to end up? she thought with a sick feeling,
and closed her eyes, trying to blot out Barbara Hutton's
lonely luxurious life.

No, she thought fiercely. That's *not* how I'll end up.
I rejected artifice when I went to Egypt after Simon and
Daddy died. I rejected materialism, status symbols and
I embraced truth, feelings, modesty.

So why am I pretending not to feel anything for
Patrick?

She felt so damned confused by what was happening
to her. And it was all so paradoxical. The attraction between herself and Patrick had sprung up out of a love
of truth. And now here Emma was, pretending not to
feel anything at all for him. The pretence sickened her.
But the thought of letting him know how she felt absolutely terrified her.

The bus rattled to a standstill suddenly.

'Here we are at the Forbes mansion!' The guide announced. 'Everybody out now, yes, yes, yes!'

Emma watched Patrick getting up, walking angrily off the bus without even glancing back at her. Her heart twisted with appalling pain. She felt such a deep sense of agony that she could barely deal with it.

But she smiled and laughed and flirted with Toby as she got off the bus and the sunlight burned her skin while pain burned her heart because she did not look at Patrick, did not even glance at him, too busy pretending and pretending and pretending...

How do I have the nerve to expect the truth from other people when I don't have the guts to live by it myself? Of course I felt something for him, of course I'm involved with him—and I knew that this morning, so why did I lie, and why am I lying still?

They all stood outside Malcolm Forbes' beautiful Arabic palace. It rose up, white and elegant, against the hot blue sky. Tall black iron gates guarded it. Fringed trees lined the black and white mosaic path.

'Rather poky, isn't it?' Natasha drawled. 'For a mansion, I mean. Not half as big as our place, is it, Charles?'

Charles looked embarrassed, and shuffled his feet. 'Darling, please don't...'

'Oh, but just look at the size of the doors, darling!' Natasha was showing off like mad. 'Our front doors are as big as——'

'Your mouth?' muttered Toby, behind her.

Natasha spun, eyes narrowing like a nasty cat's. 'I heard that.'

'Got big ears, then too, haven't you?' Toby said flatly.

'And you've got a stupid face,' Natasha hissed. 'I don't know what Emma sees in you. Maybe she doesn't see anything. Maybe I should tell everyone that you're madly in love with her.'

'And maybe I should tell everyone you were a kitchen-maid when Charles first met you, and he's failed to turn you into a lady by marrying you!'

Natasha went white with rage. 'Why, you little——'

'Which just goes to prove,' said Toby furiously, 'that money can't buy you class, good manners or intelligence.'

'You bastard!' Natasha went for him like a hissing cat. 'I'll——'

'All right, that's enough!' Patrick bit out under his breath, stepping in to tower menacingly over them all. 'If you want to indulge in family warfare, please feel free, but not while I'm around, and certainly not in public.'

'Did you hear what he said?' Natasha spat, struggling.

'Clearly,' Patrick said tightly. 'But I don't know how the hell it blew up out of nowhere. I detest public scenes and I certainly won't tolerate any on this trip. Is that clear?'

Emma kept well out of the way, standing back, embarrassed by the scene and shocked by the revelation about Natasha. No wonder she was so badly behaved and such a show-off. She clearly felt at once elevated and at the same time inferior by the position she had gained when she'd married Charles.

Studying both Natasha and Charles, she felt a great deal of sympathy for both. It was difficult to adjust to money and social status if you had never had it. And Charles clearly loved his wife. He was currently running a hand over his eyes, sighing deeply, shaking his blond head. He wasn't angry with Natasha, just exasperated.

'Charles?' Natasha glared at her husband, but her lower lip trembled, belying her temper. 'Aren't you going to defend me?'

'Darling,' Charles sighed, 'I can't keep defending you like this. Sooner or later you have to learn not to *do* that kind of thing.'

'What kind of thing?' Natasha asked, going scarlet.

Charles pushed his hands into his trouser pockets and looked helplessly at Patrick.

Patrick looked at Natasha. 'Showing off. You've been doing it all morning. I think Toby just reached the end of his tether.'

'Too right,' muttered Toby. 'Hearing her show off to *me* about the house *I* grew up in is just too much.'

A cluster of people stood around watching the expensively dressed group having an argument on the hot pavement.

'You may have grown up in it,' flared Natasha, 'but it's mine now!'

'Oh, for God's sake!'

'Natasha——'

'That's enough!' Patrick clamped an iron hand over Natasha's wrist. 'You are *definitely* spending the rest of the day with me. Charles and Toby stick together and don't embarrass me with any more public scenes, or I'll throw you all off the ship. Got it?'

Charles nodded silently.

Toby said, 'I'm spending the day with Emma.'

Patrick's blue eyes flicked to Emma's face expressionlessly. 'Fine. But try to keep him close to you, Emma. Don't let him anywhere near Natasha or me, and don't you come anywhere near us either.'

'OK.' Emma was cool and polite while her heart twisted even more savagely.

He gave a curt nod, turned on his heel, and strode into the mansion gates with Natasha trotting obediently alongside him, giving him adoring glances from under her lashes and murmuring something about loving masterful men.

How little he cares for me, Emma thought bitterly, staring after him. To actually *ask* me point-blank to keep away from him all day. To be pleased that I'm spending the day with Toby.

She thought of how he had made love to her, so many times now, since she'd boarded this wretched yacht, and she wanted to run after him, claw his eyes out, scream at him for being a callous, calculating swine.

To think I started to believe in him, she thought, horrified. To trust him, to care what he thought about me, to believe that we had something deeper in common than just a sexual attraction.

The day was going from bad to worse.

This whole thing was a nightmare.

If he didn't care for me, why did he keep his promise yesterday? she wondered. If he didn't care for me, why did he try to find out so much about me? If he didn't care for me, why did he stop making love to me when I asked him to?

But if he cared for me, why did he just do this? And ignore me? Look straight through me as though I'd never kissed him, touched him, told him intimate things about myself?

'Sorry about that,' Toby said beside her. 'You look confused and angry and upset. I didn't mean to affect you like that with such a row.'

Emma stared at him. She had forgotten he was even there.

He touched her cheek, smiling. 'Do you forgive me?'

'Of course.' She smiled back, wondering if she would go insane with the questions, the endless questions, and the terrible pain of all this. But she had to pretend it wasn't Patrick that had upset her. She had to pretend it was Toby. She hated herself but she had to pretend and pretend and pretend...

They went inside the Forbes mansion, and Emma pretended not to notice Patrick standing in one of the rooms, handsome and intelligent and desirable, talking to Natasha in a lowered, intimate voice, smiling into her pretty, pussycat face. And the more she pretended, the more hurt she felt, and the more hurt she felt, the more she pretended . . .

In the rear gardens, they all stood in separate places, surrounded by bright scarlet flowers, a black and white mosaic terrace, a swimming-pool, and the cluster of shacks and houses sliding down the hillside that was Tangier, with the sea glittering blue beyond.

'Oh, Patrick . . . !' Natasha was laughing softly, her face close to his. 'You really are a knight in shining armour to me, aren't you?'

Jealousy hit Emma like a rocket as she saw Patrick bend his head close to Natasha's and whisper something in her ear that made Natasha giggle flirtatiously and run her hand over his shoulder.

Suddenly, he lifted his head and glanced in Emma's direction. At once, she whirled away from his sight, turning to Toby as confusion began to eat away at her confidence. He couldn't be interested in Natasha— surely? She was a married woman!

And Patrick's a playboy from way back, she thought in horror. He's probably seduced plenty of married women. Nausea rose in her. She thought of her growing feelings for him and wanted to throw up.

Sweat broke out on her forehead. It can't be true. Is this how it's done? Does he concentrate everything on a woman until he either seduces her or cuts his losses and moves on?

While I'm left feeling all of this? Rage overwhelmed her. *He* started this, she thought fiercely. I didn't do anything! I was just minding my own business! He pushed at me, made me attracted to him, made me kiss him, made me feel things, feel things, feel all of this . . .

'The vile one,' Toby drawled under his breath, 'is moving in on Patrick now. I expect that's her revenge on us all.'

'Why should Patrick let her do it, though?' Emma laughed lightly with her usual brilliant pretence of not feeling a thing. 'Unless he wants her for the night or something. He is that type of man, isn't he?'

'Don't be stupid!' Toby laughed. 'Patrick's not interested in married women.'

Emma looked again at Patrick, saw him laughing intimately with Natasha, and felt riddled with rage and jealousy. He *is* that type of man. He tried to get me into bed and now he's cut his losses, moving on to get Natasha instead.

'Come on.' Toby touched her arm lightly. 'Let's pootle outside so I can buy a souvenir or two.'

Emma went with him, rage in her heart.

You fool! she thought furiously. To think you actually believed yourself in love with Patrick Kinsella! Sitting in that study like a romantic idiot, thinking about his marriage, the similarities between you, the feelings, the attraction . . . and he'd fabricated it all just to get you into bed, you stupid girl!

When they got outside, Toby ran up the street to the souvenir-sellers who had perched their wares on a dusty wall. Leaning against the black railings of the mansion, Emma struggled to keep the hot, angry tears from her eyes. Stupid tears! Stupid romantic fool, believing in a man like that—you idiot, you *idiot*!

'Look what I got!' Toby came running up to her, eyes dancing as he held up a plastic camel. 'I thought it would make an excellent present for my aunt Maud. Unfortunately, I don't have an aunt Maud. But it's the thought that counts.'

Emma saw Patrick striding out of the gates beside her, his hand on Natasha's arm.

'Oh, Toby!' Emma said with a sophisticated laugh, 'You are a hoot!' Moving closer, she kissed his cheek.

Patrick just walked coolly past without even glancing at her as she flirted openly with Toby. Emma stared after him with black, pain- and anger-filled eyes. She wanted to die. He really doesn't care ... she thought.

'Back on the bus, everybody!' The guide grinned inanely, holding his blue umbrella aloft and waving it.

Walking back on shaky legs, Emma avoided looking at Patrick, who was sitting in the front seat with Natasha beside him, and allowing Natasha to whisper vicious no things in his ear.

'Let's play with my camel,' Toby giggled, sitting down at the back with Emma.

Emma smiled but turned to stare out of the window as the bus rattled away, driving down steep slopes towards the bazaar, and soon they were bumping over unmade roads of mud and gravel, past Moroccan houses with mosque-like doors, past road signs in red and yellow Arabic script.

The bus stopped at a crossroads—or rather on a hot, dusty unmade crossroads which was largely dried mud.

'Everybody out for the wonderful bazaar!' said the guide.

Not more pretending not to care about Patrick, thought Emma with a lurch of pain in her heart, but she got off the bus, talking and flirting with Toby as though she hadn't a care in the world, while all the time she was aware of Patrick's every move, his every smile to Natasha ...

'Follow me!' The guide raised his blue umbrella as though it were a beacon of light, and led them down the muddy slope towards the bazaar while ragged children

ran at them, pleading for money, little hands
outstretched.

They entered the bazaar, a noisy, huddled jamboree
of muddy paths winding through long narrow alleys filled
with rickety wooden lean-to shops. The scent of spicy
coffee permeated the hot air, along with the jabber of
foreign voices, the occasional radio playing Arabic songs.

'Oh, what lovely silks!' Natasha said up ahead,
stopping to look.

Emma was walking too fast and bumped into Patrick,
who had stopped with Natasha.

'Sorry, darling!' Emma drawled in a light, sophisticated voice, smiling up at him, all her will-power con-
centrated on keeping her eyes free of all emotion, all
truth, all honesty. 'I was so busy talking to Toby that I
didn't notice you.'

'Not at all,' drawled Patrick, equally sophisticated and
unemotional. 'I love it when beautiful women bump into
me so prettily.'

'We're such dollies, aren't we, darling?' drawled
Emma, and as she moved past him a flash of pure jealous
pain flared in her eyes for a split-second, just a split-
second, but he saw it, he *saw* it, and she felt humiliated,
terrified, walking quickly away with Toby at her side.

Oh, my God, she thought, feeling as though she was
going to throw up. He saw it. He saw my feelings.
Perhaps he didn't, though, she told herself in panic.
Maybe he cares so little he wouldn't even notice if I threw
myself into his arms and pleaded with him not to hurt
me.

But oh, yes, he would notice! And how amused he
would be! How triumphant. How superior he would feel
to poor, romantic, foolish Emma Baccarat for falling in
love with him when he had just been playing a very
sophisticated game with her heart . . .

I'm not in love with him, she thought fiercely. I'm *not*!

'Wait a second, Toby!' Charles called from behind them in the bazaar. 'Patrick says we're going in here for a glass of mint tea.'

Emma and Toby turned to see the others waiting for them at the door to a large marble building.

'What is it?' Toby asked, walking back to his brother with Emma.

'A rug shop,' Patrick drawled. 'I'm going to take a look and maybe have one flown back for me.'

'Oh, I could buy one for my aunt Maud!'

Emma laughed in a sophisticated way, tapping his arm. 'But you don't have an aunt Maud!' And they giggled together as they entered the shop ahead of Patrick and Natasha and Charles. Emma felt desperate to prove that she didn't care at all. So she linked her arm through Toby's and smiled up at him while the pain went on and on and on...

They entered the marble shop, which indeed sold rugs as well as caftans and fez hats. They inspected a lot of rugs.

Toby bought a fez and put it on, saying, 'I am henceforth to be addressed as Abdul.'

Emma laughed and pretended not to notice Patrick stroking a strand of dark hair out of Natasha's eyes.

The guide was waiting for them in the rooftop bar, where a Moroccan band was playing strangely beautiful music while people sat around in the sun drinking hot mint tea from glasses in silver filigree holders.

Patrick sat with Natasha. Emma burned with hurt jealousy as she sat between Charles and Toby, watching Natasha continually run her hand over Patrick's.

'She's just doing it to get back at me,' Charles muttered to Toby across Emma. 'For not sticking up for her earlier. You really are a pest, Toby. I shan't bring you along again.'

Toby looked as miserable as Emma felt.

Later, they left the bar and walked to a restaurant overlooking the bazaar. Emma had to sit and watch Natasha with Patrick again. She hated the pair of them and refused to meet Patrick's piercing blue eyes, even though he kept watching her as she laughed and flirted lightly with Toby.

God help me, she kept thinking desperately under her laughter and flirtation. Get me out of here. I can't keep this up much longer. I want to cry my bloody eyes out.

At eleven, in hot darkness, they left the restaurant and went back to board the bus. It rattled back down towards the harbour with everyone still segregated by the afternoon's row.

The bus rattled on to the dirty dock, and they all disembarked while Patrick paid the rest of the money to the guide and driver. Emma walked to the yacht arm in arm with Toby.

'I'm so tired!' Emma yawned prettily as she leaned on Toby's shoulder. 'Would you mind awfully if I went straight down to bed?'

'Can I come with you?' Toby giggled. 'Can I bring my plastic camel?'

'Certainly not,' Emma said lightly. 'Goodnight, everyone!'

She walked languidly along the deck, smiling as she went, and as soon as she was on the stairs and out of sight the pain really let rip across her chest like a knife-wound.

I can barely think, she realised, stumbling into her cabin, fighting the hot tears that bit into her eyes. I can barely see. Oh, God, what the hell is happening to me?

Stripping off her clothes, she hunted blindly for a nightdress because her pyjamas were now in the washing

basket and her eyes had misted so badly with pent-up
tears that she couldn't blink them back fast enough to
see what she was doing.

She found the cool white satin nightdress in her
wardrobe. She slid it on, strappy and sensual, and as
her mouth trembled she saw herself reflected in the long
wardrobe mirror, a beautiful young woman always alone,
always alone, always, always alone...

'Patrick...!' she whispered, pushing her hands through
her hair, and the sense of loss was as inexplicable as it
was crucifying.

The knock on her cabin door made her spin, wipe her
tears away, fight for self-control, for the will-power she
needed to sound normal as she called out casually, 'Who
is it?'

'Patrick.'

She almost fell over, her heart pounding so hard she
was shaking, staring at the door, thinking, I mustn't let
him see I've been crying, mustn't let him see how I feel...

'Just a minute!' She sounded so cool, but she was
running to the bathroom in a panic, splashing cold water
on her puffy eyes, fighting to seem calm. God, she didn't
even have the old excuse any more not to let him in. He
could hardly be coming to seduce her, not now, not when
he'd already moved on to another woman, the bastard,
the bastard...

She went over to the door, taking several deep breaths,
pinning her cool, sophisticated smile to her face as she
opened the door to him.

He towered in the doorway, devastatingly gorgeous,
wearing a dark red dressing-gown that made her eyes
widen and her heart hammer.

'Hi,' he drawled with a cynical smile, holding a glass
of brandy in one long hand. 'I dropped by to bring you
this. Toby said you wanted it.'

'Did he?' She hadn't mentioned any such thing to Toby. But then, Toby might have said it as an excuse to come to her cabin—and Patrick might have misinterpreted it as a genuine request for brandy. God, this was convoluted. There were so many different avenues to explore, but at the end of them all lay the ultimate answer: he must not see how she felt.

'You don't want brandy?'

'Yes, I do.' She smiled calmly, her heart pounding. 'I'd just forgotten about it, that's all.'

He gave a hard smile. 'Right. Here—I'll just put it on the table for you.'

If she refused, he would think she was afraid. 'Thanks,' she said lightly, shrugging and holding the door open.

He strode lazily to the coffee-table while Emma loitered in the open doorway, her heart banging violently, trying to appear relaxed.

Patrick put the glass down, turned to look at her. 'Getting on well with Toby, I see.'

'He's a sweet boy.'

He laughed softly, watching her with those devastating blue eyes. 'A *sweet boy*? Is that really all you have to say about him?'

'What else can I say? I barely know him.' Her face blushed. She knew what he was implying, but he was right, and they both knew it, so what was the point in denying it?

'You knew him well enough to fling your arms around his neck and kiss him.'

'When?' she asked, her heart leaping, knowing precisely what he was talking about, every second of the day logged in her heart in painful detail.

'Outside the Forbes mansion.'

'Oh, yes...' Her eyes flashed with sudden excitement—clearly, every detail was logged in his mind too.

'Not a passionate kiss, though, was it?'

Her eyes met his in exciting silence.

'Not exactly——' he walked slowly towards her, making her pulses race like wildfire '—a kiss to set the world on fire.'

'Maybe I don't like kisses that set the world on fire.'

'You liked them well enough with me.'

'No, I fought you—remember?'

His eyes gleamed as he stopped in front of her, and the electricity crackled between them tangibly.

'Besides,' Emma said in a soft, acid-edged voice, 'I thought you were far too busy with Natasha to notice whether I kissed Toby or not. I'm surprised my kiss with him even registered in your otherwise occupied mind.'

'Surprised, but not displeased.'

She lowered her lashes with a smile.

'No good hiding those beautiful green eyes from me, Miss Baccarat.'

Emma's heart leapt in violent response to the eroticism of her formal title when used in these circumstances by this man.

'I saw the excitement in them,' Patrick murmured, 'just now.'

She was so excited that she gave a brief, breathless laugh and flashed a look up at him through her lashes.

'I also saw,' he drawled softly, meeting her gaze, 'the jealousy in them.'

Her smile froze.

'All day.' One strong hand reached out slowly to touch her thick dark hair, making her shiver. 'You were jealous of me and Natasha—weren't you? Contrary to what you said this morning, you care very much what I do.'

Emma angrily dashed his hand away from her hair, her eyes flaring with temper and humiliation. 'Is that what you've come here for? To score points off me? Is this some kind of sick game, Patrick?'

'Side-stepping the truth with a barrage of questions! What a politician you are, Emma! What happened to the woman I met, the woman who wanted the whole truth and nothing but the truth?'

'The truth, Patrick? As I see it? Is that what you really want to hear?'

'Absolutely.'

'You tried and failed to get me into bed, then turned your very potent sexual weapons on Natasha! If I appeared to be jealous, it was because I was so angry about what you had done that I wanted to stick a knife in you! And who can blame me? Look at the way you've behaved! Chasing me like that, bludgeoning me towards the bedroom—then dumping me for Natasha——'

'I'm not after Natasha! She's a married woman!'

'I'm sure that wouldn't stop a man like you!'

'Then why am I here, with you, in your cabin,' he demanded harshly, 'instead of three doors away, with Natasha, in mine?'

'I don't know. Maybe it's too risky, with Charles around.'

'Charles is my favourite cousin. I wouldn't betray him like that.'

'Then why did you spend the whole day,' she asked through her teeth, 'flirting with his wife, right in front of him?'

'To make you jealous!' he bit out thickly, and her heart stopped beating with abrupt violence as she stared into his blue eyes in disbelief.

'I don't believe you!'

'Don't you, by God!' His eyes were hot, his face darkly flushed as he reached for her, gripping her waist. 'Then let me prove it to you!'

'With a kiss?' Emma struggled angrily in his arms. 'Go to hell! I know precisely what a kiss from you will lead to if I let it!'

'Yes, so do I!' He breathed harshly as he pulled her hard against him and heard her gasp of exquisite pleasure at the contact with his powerful body. 'That's precisely why I'm going to do it. To force you to acknowledge just how strong——'

'Don't!'

'Just how strong the bond between us really is.'

Emma stopped struggling, heart banging hard, hands clutching his broad shoulders. 'What bond...? There is no bond...'

'There is and you know it.'

'Then put a name on it!' Her voice was raw, husky, filled with emotion as she stared up into his eyes. 'For God's sake make it logical before I go completely crazy!'

He held her, breathing hard. 'Is it affecting you that deeply, Emma?'

Her eyes closed. 'Yes...does that make you feel good?'

'It certainly does,' he said thickly, staring, 'because it affects me that deeply too.'

She looked up into his eyes, feeling a rush of emotion so strong it was like floodgates opening to let dammed-up hot water cascade in drowning torrents across her heart.

Patrick caught his breath at the look on her face. 'Oh, God...!' he whispered hoarsely, and a second later his mouth was burning on hers as he crushed her hard against him.

She went willingly. More than willingly. Her arms wrapped around his strong neck, her mouth was fiercely responsive beneath his, and he gripped her very tightly, harsh sounds of excitement coming from the back of his throat as he pressed her body against his.

Patrick groaned, fumbled behind him for the light switch, plunged them both into darkness, then picked her up in his arms and strode to the bed, almost falling on to it with her.

CHAPTER EIGHT

EMMA'S lashes flickered damp against her hot cheek-bones. In the darkness, they kissed frenziedly, and outside the moonlight played silver on the dark blue waves as the ship sailed across the Moroccan coast towards Casablanca.

Patrick slid on top of her in his dressing-gown, his mouth pressed to hers, groans of pleasure coming from the back of his throat as his hands moved in her silken hair, slid over her naked throat, moved down caressingly to her breasts.

Emma arched to meet them. She was fire and air, whispering his name in a hoarse, drugged voice, kissing him fiercely as they exploded together into that other dimension only they could share, that other world where love transcended sex, made every movement of their hot, excited, tense bodies just an expression of emotion through the flesh.

It didn't feel like sex. It felt like the absolute necessity to mate, lion with lioness, an affirmation of life.

Her nightdress was sliding down in his strong hands, baring her breasts, the nipples hard as his fingers stroked them, stroked them, slowly and carefully, firmly and commandingly, stroking, stroking, stroking until he bent his dark head, her hands in his hair, and his hot mouth closed over her aching nipple.

'Oh ... oh ...' Emma twisted beneath him, knowing suddenly that he was not going to rush, that he was going to build her up, higher and higher, with excitement, the expertise he had accumulated over the years something she not only wanted but actively needed in order to reach the pleasure only he was capable of unleashing in her.

Their mouths exchanged love and heat in lingering kisses, and as she moaned softly his hands were moving down to her thighs, slowly spreading them and making her whimper as those strong fingers moved up and down, very slowly, very firmly, up and down her inner thighs.

'Patrick...' she whispered, aching for his touch, and when she felt his fingers slide to the wet, slippery apex of her body she moaned loudly, her mouth against his, gasping as she felt one strong finger move slowly inside her, pause motionless, so motionless that she moaned again and began to move herself against his palm, flexing pelvic muscles she never knew she had, her legs spreading wider, wider, wider...

He groaned then, and buried his hot mouth in her throat, kissing her, whispering wicked things against her shivering skin as his hand worked slowly, sensuously, stroking her to a new plateau of excitement.

Her silk nightdress was rucked up around her waist, rucked down to bare her breasts. It might just as well not have been there at all, for she felt nude, her skin very hot, and the combination of his mouth suddenly sucking at her nipple while his hand moved slowly between her thighs made her want to cry out as excitement escalated.

Suddenly, her own hands were moving over him, slowly pulling the dressing-gown he wore aside, touching his chest, hearing him catch his breath with excitement as her hands moved lower, lower, lower...

'Yes!' he said, as though she had spoken, and his hips jutted forward in excruciating excitement, waiting for her touch, aching for it as much as she had for his. 'Oh, God...!'

Emma's fingers slid like soft butterflies on to the hard-veined flesh, and his cry of agonised pleasure made her moan as she met his mouth, kissing him deeply as she stroked him.

It was so many years since she had touched a man that she was afraid to do it wrong, to make a fool of herself, to be inept, inadequate, and her fear made her hesitate, eyes flying open to stare at him in the darkness, see the taut excitement on his face as her fingers fell away from him.

He opened his eyes, breathing harshly, stared at her. 'What...? Did I hurt you? Is something wrong?'

'I...' She felt so exposed, not just physically but emotionally, and began—to her horror—to stammer her answer like a schoolgirl. 'I—I just feel so... I mean, I haven't done this for so long, I——' She broke off, flushing scarlet with humiliated confusion, then tried again. 'I don't know what to do—or—or how to—to——'

'Darling, it's OK,' Patrick said with a tenderness that was moving. 'You don't need to do anything to arouse me, nothing at all. Leave it all to me. I don't expect any kind of display from you, or expertise or——'

'But I feel so hopeless!' The words flew from her as her flush deepened and she closed her eyes, burying her face in her own shoulder, refusing to look at him now that the truth was out about her ineptitude and her fear. 'I never was particularly good at this sort of thing. I was always playing at it with Simon—my husband. I was like an actress, pretending to be brilliant, doing everything I was supposed to—and faking my own pleasure like mad.' She couldn't stop the words flooding out of her now, with that odd combination of anger and humility. 'And I promised myself I'd never lie again. Not in any way, shape or form. How can I lie now?' Her voice grew huskier than it had ever been before as she bravely raised her eyes to meet his. 'Here with you?'

'But you're not lying—are you?' he said deeply. 'You haven't faked excitement with me once.'

'No, but I—I—feel self-conscious about touching you.' God, this was so honest, so personal, she felt completely vulnerable, more than she ever had in her life.

'Then don't try to touch me, darling,' he whispered, 'until you feel able to.'

She looked up into his eyes, aware of the deepening of their relationship, and the fresh rawness of honesty it was bringing into play between them.

'It may take a very long time,' Patrick said gently, 'for you to be able to touch me as freely as I touch you. But it really doesn't matter that much to me. It's not what's most important to me.'

Emma moistened her lips, studying him in the darkness. 'What *is* most important to you, Patrick?'

The blue eyes seemed to glitter like *Starry Night* again, and she felt weak with love as she looked into them, saw the wariness, the suspicion, followed by the determination to retain their mutual honesty, and finally—the decision to trust her.

'It's difficult,' he said deeply, 'to answer that in one sentence. There are so many things that are very important to me. Trust, for instance, and loyalty. Integrity, too. And a capacity for not only seeing but speaking the truth.'

'Back to the truth, then?' she said huskily, smiling.

'What else is there? You see, I spent most of my early life trapped by lies and pretence. I had to smash the whole edifice to pieces in order to be free, and now that I am free I intend to stay that way, so you must never lie to me, Emma, or you'll lose me.'

Her heart skipped beats. 'I—I didn't know I had you.'

'What do you think I'm doing here,' he murmured, kissing her mouth lingeringly, 'lying naked in bed with you, seriously aroused, not forcing you to make love?'

Her lashes flickered as she smiled, kissing him back.

Patrick studied her in the darkness. 'You must also be beginning to trust me, or I wouldn't be here with you like this.'

It was her turn to tense, eyes shooting up to his. 'I...' She felt her mind move rapidly for the most concise and unromantic answer possible. 'I think this has happened more out of a series of difficult emotional reactions than anything else.'

'Such as...?'

'I...' She was flushed and afraid of revealing too much. 'I felt rather pushed today, first telling you that I didn't care about you, then having to watch you with Natasha. And also...' She hesitated, heart drumming like mad, then blurted out, 'Also, I had a conversation with Liz in your study that made me—made me...' She broke off, angry with herself for being so afraid of revealing her feelings.

'What conversation with Liz?' He frowned, and his body was heavy and hot on hers, still pulsing with excited blood, even though they had paused for this brief hiatus. 'What did she say?'

'She told me about your marriage.'

He caught his breath, watching her, face immobile. Then he expelled his breath, looked briefly away. 'I see...'

Emma cleared her throat. 'Is there some reason why you didn't tell me about your marriage before?'

'Yes,' he drawled, smiling sardonically, not looking at her.

The ship moved through the dark waters of the Med, and the moonlight danced in silver patterns on the wall of the dark cabin where Emma and Patrick lay naked together.

'Well?' she asked huskily. 'Are you going to refuse to talk about it now that I've confronted you with it?'

He looked down at her, his face wry. 'I'd rather not talk about it right now, if that's what you mean. But I'll certainly agree to discuss it with you at a later date.'

Her face shuttered. 'I see,' she said coldly, feeling hurt.

'No, I don't think you do, Emma,' he drawled, 'and I can't explain it, not now, not like this.' He moved his hard, hot body against hers, closing his eyes, sliding his mouth against her throat, whispering thickly, 'I'm too excited. I've stopped to talk, but I can't stop forever, not when I want you this much.'

'I can't let you make love to me, Patrick!'

'Yes, you can...' His mouth closed over hers in a deep, drugging kiss, and she stupidly let him kiss her, because she loved the feel of his mouth, his body, his hands.

The fire rushed between them suddenly, making them both stir and moan with excitement, and she felt his long fingers sliding back along her inner thighs, sliding slowly but surely to the fierce wet heat.

Shameful desire burned her, made the nub of flesh between her thighs prickle and sting. He touched it cleverly, so cleverly that she cried out and let him stroke it some more because he did it so well, as though he knew every nerve-ending, every response, and she had never been touched so expertly that it seemed criminal to refuse to let him take her where she so badly needed to go: ecstasy.

The truth is, she thought as excitement escalated between them, the truth is that I *want him*, and suddenly the truth had never been so dangerous to follow through to its natural conclusion.

Her hands were moving over him, over that magnificent body that strained against her, answering her own desire. She could feel the blood beating under his hot skin, could feel the excited heat of his breathing on her own skin, and could very definitely feel the hard pulsation of his manhood pushing against her spread thighs.

'No,' she whispered in husky excitement, 'I won't let you make love to me, Patrick. Why should I trust you?'

'I won't let you down,' he groaned against her mouth, pushing his body against her, his heart banging hard. 'I've never wanted a woman as much as this. Quite apart from that, I respected your mind before I even desired your body. I think I can promise I'll feel even more for you if you let me make love to you.'

'But *I'll* feel frightened and unsure.'

'Oh, God, darling, please . . .' He moved with a rough exclamation, breathing harder, heart beating faster, and his finger still stroked her as she felt the first exquisite press of his manhood against that burning, wet entrance to her body. 'Emma . . . Emma . . .'

'Don't, Patrick!' She pushed at his bare chest in panic, eyes wild in the hot darkness. 'How can I possibly let you make love to me like this? How can I possibly believe you really do respect me when you've told me almost nothing personal about yourself?'

'Now isn't the time . . .'

'Then when is the time?'

'Don't stop me now . . . don't . . .'

'You won't even tell me about your first wife!' she cried in desperation as his fingers bit into her hips, his powerful body positioned between her thighs, poised for entry. 'In fact, you didn't tell me about her in the first place—your sister did!'

He stopped, breathing hard, sweat on his brow. 'Emma . . . I'm on the edge here . . . don't stop me, please . . .'

Emma breathed hard too, just as fiercely aroused, yet held back by her even more fierce emotions. He was right; he really was on the edge. She could feel the pulse of hot blood in his manhood, the overriding need for release. She knew suddenly that he was almost beyond stopping, and the fear that flooded her was nearly as great as the dawn of understanding for the differences in their bodies.

But if he cared for her at all he would stop.

No matter how close he was to the edge, no matter how far she had stupidly allowed him to go, and no matter how badly he wanted her—if he cared for her, he would stop.

And she knew she only had to ask.

She knew it with such a deep certainty that in that split-second of danger she had nothing but her faith in him.

It was a faith she had always had, right from the start, but which she had been refusing to face out of fear of just what that faith meant; for it could only be love.

'Darling...' he groaned, taking her silence for submission, and began to enter her with a hoarse gasp of excitement.

'If you want to prove you care for me,' she blurted out in a raw panic, 'you won't do this.'

He stared down at her dazedly. 'Emma...'

'I mean it, Patrick,' she whispered. 'It's the only way to prove conclusively, once and for all, that you really aren't just a playboy, and that you really do care for me. But if you go ahead with this, if you take me now, then I'll have no choice but to believe you want nothing from me but sex.'

He closed his eyes briefly, dragging air into his lungs, and she lay beneath him, sprawled in naked vulnerability, fear and excitement, the throbbing ache between her thighs urging her to mate uninhibitedly with him, while the throbbing ache in her heart demanded love.

'I can surely prove I care,' he said thickly, 'by staying with you until and beyond the end of the cruise.'

'It's not quite so symbolic, though, is it?' Her husky voice had never sounded so completely female in its absolute vulnerability and hope. 'A cynical playboy staying with me while getting sex? That's not as moving as a cynical playboy drawing back from the edge for the sake of a woman he cares about.'

He closed his eyes again, whispering something under his breath.

'Patrick——' she kissed his strong throat '—I'm sorry to ask it of you. But it's the only way I'll ever be able to trust you.'

'Yes, all right,' he said under his breath, and then clenched his teeth to look at her, his blue eyes suddenly steely. 'But it had better not be a trick, Emma, or I'll——'

'It's not a trick.'

'And how the hell can I be sure of that?'

'Because you know how badly I want you to make love to me, so it's something of a sacrifice for me too.' Slowly, invitingly, she slid her body against his, making him tense like a bowstring, a fierce cry of agonised excitement coming from the back of his throat.

'Oh, God, don't move like that!' His eyes blazed open like blue fire. 'Are you completely out of your mind? Don't you know how close I am to just pinning you down and taking what I want?'

'I'm sorry, I thought——'

'I can see what you thought!' he bit out. 'That you could play with me, build me up then shoot me down in flames! Well, I'll shoot *you* down—how do you like that?'

'No, please——'

'Give me one good reason why I shouldn't!' His hands were gripping her hips, his body ready to take possession.

'To prove you really do care for——'

'Right now that doesn't seem like a good enough reason!'

'Patrick, please, I——'

'Give me a good reason!' he bit out harshly as she felt his throbbing manhood burn just inside her in demanding hunger. 'And give it quickly!'

Tears stung her eyes suddenly. 'I'll never forgive you! I'll never forgive you! I mean it, Patrick, I'll never forgive you!'

With a snarled obscenity, he withdrew and flung himself down on the bed beside her, one arm above his head, staring up at the darkened ceiling with a face like thunder.

Emma felt the hot tears slide over her lashes as she realised how close she had come to being taught a very dangerous lesson, and how very much she owed him for being man enough to draw back. Trembling, she pulled her body back into a less vulnerable position, and slid next to him to kiss his neck with gratitude.

'Don't push it!' he said tightly, but he looked at her out of the corner of his eye, and gave an irritable shrug which placed his strong arm firmly around her shoulders. 'Come on. Snuggle up and go to sleep. But don't bloody well touch or kiss me, or you'll find yourself pinned down in seconds.'

'Are you—are you planning to sleep here?'

'No. But I want to wait until you're asleep before I go back to my cabin. I'm much too aroused to think about going back to sleep alone when I could be next to your delectably naked body instead. Just don't press it against me too much. You won't escape a second time.'

Emma went pale, dragged the coverlets up over them both, and lay tense against him in silence for a long time. She wanted desperately to ask him a million questions. Her heart was singing with love, unable to believe her faith in him truly had been justified, but here it was, the proof—he had had her precisely where he wanted her, and what had stopped him taking her was that final threat, that she would never forgive him if he did.

He really made a sacrifice then, she thought blissfully.
And how can I possibly accuse him of wanting nothing
but sex again? After this?

If he felt nothing but desire, he would have taken me
just then, because he most certainly would have been
able to. It's not as though I'm a virgin who would be
destroyed if he took me. I'm a widow, experienced and
capable of coping—just about—if he insisted.

He must also be in considerable physical discomfort
now, she realised with a frown. It occurred to her, very
excitingly, that she could ease that physical discomfort,
but although she was very tempted she knew it would
only provoke him.

Then it occurred to her that he could ease his own
discomfort, by going back to his cabin in a temper, to
touch himself and hate her. Yet he chose to stay here,
lying with his arm around her, staying close.

The extent of his involvement finally reached her.

In the darkness, she stared at the powerful wall of his
chest, and knew suddenly, without a shred of doubt,
that he *did* care for her, that he *did* respect her, and that
he *did* feel something more for her than desire.

She wanted desperately to sit up and talk to him then,
but of course she was afraid to, just in case she was
wrong, or in case he got nasty and told her to stop
tempting him.

So she lay there beside him, closed her eyes, and
dreamed of all the things they could mean to each other
if he really was sincere.

Romance blossomed in her starved mind. She could
smell the freedom of a sunlit paradise, see herself walking
hand in hand, naked, like Adam and Eve, with Patrick,
and feel the warm breeze in her hair.

Was love really real? Was it possible that a man she
loved could love her too, and that their love could be

true? That there would be no lies, no artifice, no fear and no pretence?

Oh, she couldn't believe that...

Could she...?

When she woke up, it was broad daylight, Patrick was snoring gently, and sunlight had flooded the cabin. Blinking sleepily, she heard gulls crying outside, and then realised the ship wasn't moving.

She shifted, her legs entangled with his, and he stirred.

'Mmm...' He breathed in the scent of her, sleepily opened his eyes, stared for a second, then smiled, saying huskily, 'How did I wind up in bed with you, gorgeous?'

'You obviously didn't make it back to your cabin last night.' Emma laughed softly, kissed his sleepy mouth, and he rolled over on top of her, blue eyes gleaming with a mixture of love and desire as he kissed her slowly, deeply, tenderly.

'I'm glad I stayed,' he murmured as he kissed her. 'I'd like to wake up next to you forever...'

Forever...

Her heart sang. Oh, this couldn't be happening. She felt so warm, feminine, relaxed and loved. She felt breathless and dizzy and trusting, and all the things women were supposed to feel when they fell in love...

Their mouths kissed like affectionate chipmunks, and they laughed softly to each other, eyes dancing, childlike in their sudden uncomplicated expression of love.

'Kiss, kiss, kiss...' he said softly, playing with her hair. 'I haven't felt so affectionate for years.'

'Neither have I,' she confessed, equally softly. 'And I thought we were such a pair of terrible cynics!'

'Well, you know what they say. There's nothing quite so cynical as a disillusioned romantic.'

She flushed delicately. 'I—yes, I was thinking that just the other day.'

'I've been thinking it since I met you, Emma.'

Her eyes looked deeply, trustingly into his, and his were equally serious, equally trusting.

'You know,' she confided huskily, 'I can hardly believe I'm lying here naked with you, and feeling so good about it.'

'Neither can I. I thought I'd never sleep all night with a woman I wanted without making love to her——' his smile touched her heart '—and then feel pleased about it in the morning!'

'I guess we've both broken some rules, then.'

'We have from the very beginning.'

They studied each other in silence for a long time, then his mouth slowly met hers in warm, tender love.

But suddenly his kiss took on a more adult feel, and as excitement sprang between them their bodies pressed together. His was warm, hard, and she let her pelvis slide against him, making her heart beat harder as she heard his groan of appalled desire.

'Will you let me make love to you,' he asked unsteadily, 'or is this just another lack of common sense on your part?'

'It—it's just a lack of common sense, I suppose,' she said huskily.

'Hmm.' The blue eyes studied her flushed, sleepy face. 'Well, at least it's an indication that you're not averse to making love first thing in the morning.'

She flushed pink, lowering her lashes, her fingers playing with his broad chest, then suddenly noticed again how still the ship was. 'What time are we supposed to arrive at Casablanca? I thought it wasn't until midday.'

'It's not,' he said, then tensed, eyes shooting to the window as the realisation hit him. 'Oh, hell and damnation!' He scrambled off her, naked and magnificent, the sun gleaming on his bronzed body as he strode to the window and wrenched back the curtains.

The dock of Casablanca confronted him in all its hot, dusty glory, buildings towering into the azure blue sky as the city rose up above the motionless, anchored yacht.

Turning, he strode back to the bed, snatched up his dark red dressing-gown and began dragging it on. 'They'll have been down to my cabin to try and get me. They'll know we slept together. Damn!' He ran a hand through his dark hair as she stared at him in horror, then strode to the door, tugging the belt of his robe tight. 'You'd better get up and get dressed. I'll rush off and do the same. Meet you on deck in ten minutes. And Emma——' he opened the door, looked back at her, face tough '—leave the talking to me. If you get up on deck first—don't say *anything*.'

The door slammed behind him.

Startled, Emma just sat in bed for a second, staring at the closed door and realising the extent of what had happened. They would all know. He was right.

Suddenly, she scrambled off the bed, running around like a chicken with no head, rushing to the bathroom, stripping off and leaping into the shower without hesitation, then minutes later emerging dripping and breathless to brush her teeth and then run into the cabin, semi-blow-dry her hair, hunt around madly for clothes.

What would she say to them? To Liz, to Natasha, to all of them? She winced as she tugged on silk lingerie, hunted for a sundress, her hands trembling with adrenalin-rush.

And what would they all think of her? They wouldn't understand the deep romanticism of her night with Patrick. They would simply think she was... Because of course she couldn't possibly tell them that she hadn't made love with Patrick—and even if she did tell them they'd never believe her. They'd just give her knowing smiles and giggle among themselves.

And, to make matters worse, Patrick had said he was going to do the talking. So what was he going to say? She winced at the thought of that, but as she glanced at her watch she saw she had spent too long getting dressed—it was now fifteen minutes since Patrick had left her cabin, and he must already be up on deck with the others.

Emma practically broke her neck racing out of the cabin to get there and find out what he was saying.

The deck was hot as Hades, sun burning like an oven on her bare skin, and even the blue cheesecloth sundress she wore seemed like too much in this heat.

They all sat clustered around the chairs and tables and parasols at the end of the deck while Patrick stood in front of them, talking, a glass of iced coffee in one strong hand. He looked fabulously gorgeous. He was wearing dark trousers, a black shirt, and dark glasses.

That golden romantic faith exploded in her heart like sunlight again, and she suddenly loved him so much, was so sure that he loved her, that she felt weak with emotion—and stumbled as she walked.

They heard her footfall, turned to see her approach.

'Congratulations!' Liz leapt up, resplendent in a bright purple sundress and straw hat, running towards her with arms outstretched. 'I'm so happy for both of you, I can hardly contain myself!'

Emma stared at her, and was engulfed in a frenzied embrace a moment later which knocked Liz's straw hat askew. What on earth did she mean—congratulations? Just because she and Patrick had spent the night together? It was almost in bad taste to congratulate her!

'Oh, I'm so glad he chose you!' Liz kissed her cheek, further baffling and bewildering her. 'And over the moon that it happened right under my nose, here on board! I just *knew* there was something serious going on between you two!'

'Oh...yes...' Emma was breathless, staring at Patrick over Liz's head, horror in her eyes.

Patrick just smiled at her, and the dark glasses hid his eyes so that she could not see the expression in them.

'Yes.' Natasha got up and walked towards her with a tight smile. 'I suppose we should all congratulate Miss Baccarat. It can't be easy reeling in a big fish like Patrick Kinsella in just three days. Better women than you, my dear, have tried and failed.'

Emma's eyes darted. 'Tried and failed to do what?'

'And rest assured,' Natasha said spitefully, 'that none of us thinks for one second you're marrying him for his money.'

Emma gasped, eyes shooting to Patrick's as the penny dropped with a resounding crash.

'We're going into Rabat today,' Patrick said swiftly, striding over to her side, 'to buy the ring.'

She gaped up at him in speechless shock.

'Just smile, darling!' he murmured softly in her ear. 'And don't contradict me in public or I'll kill you.'

Automatically, she pinned a tight, brittle smile on her face, but inside she was spinning like a top, conflicting emotions fighting for supremacy.

It was so romantic... a proposal of marriage... from him, from *him*! He did love her after all, then, and she hadn't imagined the beauty of their night together, or the golden sunlight that had flooded them both this morning as they'd kissed with warm, childlike romanticism and tenderness.

But years of ingrained disbelief in love—years of hurt, of disappointment, of bitter disillusion—came spinning up in rage to shout, He's just using you! He doesn't love you, and he doesn't want to marry you. He just can't think of any other way to get you into bed.

After all, we've only just met. How can he possibly mean to marry me? He's just going to spin this false

engagement out while we're on the cruise, she thought
angrily, then gradually soft-pedal his way out of it once
he's got what he wants.

'Here are the cars!' Toby called. 'Shall we go? We can
always have a jolly drunken celebration tonight for
Patrick and Emma!'

'Good idea!' Charles called, waving his sunhat. 'Shall
we say eight o'clock for cocktails back here on deck?'

'Perfect,' drawled Patrick, his arm tight around
Emma's rigid shoulders as he waved his free hand in a
casual wave. 'Have a good day!'

'Oh, it's all so romantic!' sobbed Liz, running off after
Toby and Charles.

As soon as they had gone, Emma turned to him furiously, terrified of letting any romanticism through, so
frightened that she would be humiliated by him. 'How
could you do that? What on earth posssessed you?'

He tensed, face cold and remote, head held high.
'What was I supposed to do?'

Emma went rigid, seeing his lack of love, of warmth,
of trust. It only made her even more angry and hostile
towards him as pain seeped into her bruised heart. 'I
don't know! Anything rather than stir up a phoney marriage proposal! What the hell are we going to do now?
We can't possibly go through with it!'

'We'll have to,' he said tightly, growing colder and
more remote, that cutting, sophisticated drawl coming
back into his voice. 'I've announced it now. I'm certainly not going back on it publicly.'

Her eyes blazed with terrible pain. 'You could try
telling them all the truth!'

'What—that I slept all night in your bed and didn't
make love to you?' His hard mouth curled in a contemptuous sneer. 'Are you out of your mind? I'm not
telling them I did that! That little witch Natasha would
spread it all round London, New York, Paris and

Munich! The newspapers might even get hold of it, and then I'd really be held up to scorn and ridicule! What's the matter with you? Can't you think about anyone but yourself?'

'You're not the one they'll laugh at if this engagement gets broken off the minute we leave the ship!' Her voice was icy with rigid contempt. 'All they'll see is me sleeping with you night after night, then getting dumped the minute the cruise is over. If you seriously think I'm letting you do that to me, you're in need of a lobotomy!'

'And if you think I'm going to let you humiliate me,' he said with cold, cutting contempt, 'by backing out of this engagement publicly, *you* are going to *get* a lobotomy—from me. Am I making myself clear?'

They bristled, staring at each other like a savage lion and lioness, each ready to kill the other rather than back down.

'You can't make me pretend to be about to marry you,' she said icily.

'Oh, can't I?' He towered threateningly over her, every inch of his powerful body telling her that he intended to do just that.

'No! In fact, I think the only way out of this for both of us is if I just leave this ship now, and fly back to——'

'Not while I'm around to stop you, physically, if I have to.' He took her wrist in an implacable, iron grip. 'Now come on. My car is waiting, we're driving into Rabat to buy the ring, and we will discuss the eventual outcome on the way.'

Emma struggled, but he really meant business, and he had no difficulty whatever dragging her after him with a face like granite, striding off the ship, down the gangplank towards the gleaming red car awaiting them.

'I'm not going through with this!' she said furiously.

'Shut up and get in!' he bit out, thrusting her into the car, slamming the door, then striding round to the driver's side.

Emma glared at him hotly, hating him, feeling hoaxed, conned, humiliated. Last night had meant nothing to him. He had just done it in order to win points with her. This marriage proposal was nothing but a way of forcing her hand.

She would never forgive him.

And she would never forgive herself for being such a silly, romantic little fool...

CHAPTER NINE

RABAT was the most beautiful, exotic city Emma had seen since her weeks in Egypt. It rose out of the desert in clean, shining white glory, an oasis of palm trees, luxurious buildings, busy streets, expensive hotels, the king's palace nestling in the heart of it with its long white colonnades.

Patrick stopped the car outside a wickedly expensive jeweller's and turned off the engine, glancing expressionlessly at her.

Emma looked at the glittering façade of the jeweller's. 'I've told you—I'm not going through with this.'

'We've spent the whole journey doing nothing but argue, and I'm sick to death of it. There's no way out for either of us, so stop bothering to try and find one.' He got out of the car, face hard, and strode round to her side, opening the door. 'Come on. Out you get.'

'No.' She looked at him with cold mutiny.

His mouth tightened. Then he took her arm in a hard grip and forcibly levered her out to stand beside him.

Cars whizzed past on the hot, exotic street. All the buildings were clean, beautiful, surrounded by palm trees and sunlight. The sky was achingly blue.

'Would you prefer to walk across the road with me?' Patrick drawled coldly, towering over her formidably. 'Or shall I just carry you while you kick, scream and shout obscenities?'

'I'll walk,' she said through her teeth, and crossed the road with a stylish sway, her dark head held high. Patrick strode beside her, a hard smile on his mouth.

149

The gold glass door of the jeweller's glittered in the sunlight, making her think of doors opening in her mind, door after door after door letting Patrick Kinsella walk effortlessly through, not even having to knock, or use a key, or ask for permission to enter, because each door swung open of its own accord before he reached it, and she could see him now, strolling through her mind with his hands in his pockets and a cool, calm look on his handsome face—deliberately using her vulnerability to exploit her.

What a callous, calculating swine he was.

Patrick pushed open the door and she went inside, hating him.

The atmosphere was at once reminiscent of Cartier's or Tiffany's: a deep-pile green carpet on the long, elegant floor, trays of wickedly expensive jewels, watches and rings nestling on black velvet, and a tall, inscrutably dignified Moroccan man in a smart black suit sweeping up to greet them.

'An engagement ring,' Patrick said with cool authority, pushing his hands into the pockets of his expensive black trousers and towering over the man. 'An emerald, I think. What can you show us?'

Emma prickled angrily at Patrick's cool authority and the way he displayed it, that perfect English accent, the weapon of superiority, and the calm accentuation of the whole effect in every inch of his face and body. He really was her ideal man—so much for ideals. What a lot of romantic rubbish it had all turned out to be.

The man bowed low, then whisked them to a private room, and had several trays of emeralds in various settings brought to them.

Patrick eyed a fantastic emerald and diamond necklace, smiling as he transferred it from the box to his hands, then put it around her slender white throat.

'You're not going to buy me that!' Emma said in icy fury.

'No, but it does suit you.' He watched it glitter like fire, then leaned forward and kissed her mouth. 'And I probably would buy it for you if I didn't know damned well you'd refuse it.'

He removed the necklace from her throat, and she realised how incredibly rich he must be, something that had not properly permeated her consciousness since she'd met him—she'd been too busy noticing *him*.

He was looking at emerald rings now, and she was horrified to see him selecting huge stones set in platinum or gold, surrounded by tiny diamonds.

Quickly, she looked for the smallest, cheapest ring and said, 'This one will be fine.'

Patrick eyed it with contempt. 'I think not.' He reached out and his eyes gleamed as he picked up a square-cut emerald of horrific size, set in gold, surrounded by diamonds. 'This is far more suitable.'

'No!' she said at once, blanching. 'It's much too expensive!'

'I can afford it.' His voice was as cold and cutting as those precious stones. 'Try it on.'

'No.' She withheld her hand.

His eyes narrowed. 'Don't be tiresome.'

'I'm not being tiresome, I'm being practical.'

'You're being bloody-minded.' He took her hand and forced the ring on to her finger where it glittered breathtakingly. 'I'm not having my future wife wandering around with a pathetic engagement ring.'

Her eyes flared with bitter hostility and pride. 'I'm not your future wife!'

'Nobody else knows that, Emma,' he said tightly, 'but they'll guess if we don't come back with an engagement ring fit for a queen. Now just shut up and tell me if the damned thing fits!'

She felt it angrily, her face hectic. 'Yes, it fits.'

'We'll take it.' He got to his feet, took a black wallet from his back pocket, flipped it open and selected a platinum Am Ex card from a dazzling array of every credit card in the world. 'Leave it on her finger and give me the box.'

They left the shop a few minutes later, and the ring felt heavy on her finger as she walked with a tight, set face to the car across the hot, busy street with him.

'Don't sulk.'

'I'm not sulking,' she said angrily, 'I'm angry, and have every right to be! How dare you do this? Announcing our engagement, forcing me to accept it, buying me this ridiculous bauble!'

'It's a beautiful ring.'

'It's a way to buy my silence—and my bed!'

'You think I'm trying to buy you?' His eyes flared with answering anger. 'My God, you really know how to make me lose my temper! I could easily have taken you last night.'

'But I didn't let you take me—did I, Patrick?'

'I stopped for your sake!'

They were crossing the road angrily.

'Oh, for my sake! I'm so flattered! But spending a lot of money on my phoney engagement ring would certainly help tip the scales!'

'I don't have to shell out so much as fifty cents to get you into bed, and you know it!'

Emma's eyes blazed with furious pride and her hand came shooting up to slap him hard on the face. He caught her by the wrist, stopping her. They glared at each other in the middle of the road, both bristling with hatred.

A car hooted angrily at them.

'You're going to get us killed!' Patrick bit out thickly, and dragged her over to the car, pushing her into the front seat, then getting in beside her.

'I'll never let you touch me again!' Emma said in hurt fury as he started the car. 'Never—do you hear me?'

'Loud and clear.' With a screech of tyres, he drove into the glittering stream of traffic.

Emma looked down at her ring through a haze of angry emotion. Light and colour blazed from it—bright green, emerald-green, the colour of Ireland...

She thought of their days together, of the build-up of feeling, of the culmination of it last night, and the love she had felt this morning as she'd lain in his arms, believing, for one brief, shining moment, in love.

How she hated him. It seemed more bitterly hurtful to have her hopes destroyed this time than it had ever been before. She suddenly wondered if she would ever recover, if she would ever trust a man again, and the magnitude of her feelings suddenly hit her like a hail of gunfire.

I'm in love with him, she thought, and hot tears blazed into her eyes, stinging, hurting, choking her throat with emotion.

Patrick parked at a stunning hotel. 'We'll have lunch here.'

'And then go back to the ship,' she said tightly, 'to let everyone know the engagement is cancelled.'

'We will not, Emma!' He looked at her with blazing eyes. 'Now stop fighting me and start accepting it!'

'How can I do that? You know as well as I do that we can't possibly marry each other!'

'Why not?' he said cuttingly, astonishing her, making her stare at his hard profile as he turned away from her and got out of the car.

What had he just said? Why not? She stared as he strode round to her side, opened the door, watched her in formidable silence, waiting to see if she'd get out by herself or be dragged out by him.

'Did you just say why not?' Emma asked coldly, stepping out of the car, still staring.

'Yes.' He slammed the door, took her arm in a hard grip, and marched her into the hotel, which had a ravishing mosaic courtyard, where expensively coiffed women drank iced coffee amid the fountains and the palm trees.

He led a speechless Emma to a long, luxurious couch.

'Stop pushing me around,' she muttered, sitting down with a hostile expression on her face while he sat beside her on the couch. 'And kindly explain your very cryptic remark to me.'

'It's perfectly simple,' he drawled, and he had never sounded more remote, cool, sophisticated, blasé. 'We get on, we fancy each other, and we're both single. Why not go through with this phoney marriage?'

She stared, her mouth open. 'I can't believe you said that.'

Patrick gave a cynical laugh, and a second later a white-liveried waiter appeared to take their order of iced coffee and a large platter of Moroccan meats.

'So,' Patrick said coolly, eyeing her, 'what do you think? Shall we just go through with it and see what happens?'

'No, we damned well will not!'

'Strong words.' He laughed sardonically, sliding his dark glasses off to let his blue eyes mock her. 'But I think it's a reasonably sensible solution. After all, we're both cynical and——'

'I'm not marrying a man on that basis!'

'What other basis would you marry on?'

Her eyes blazed with angry emotion. 'Love!'

'I thought you didn't believe in love?'

At once she looked away, caught by his cleverness, her face white and her eyes horrified.

'Hmm?' He was watching her shrewdly. 'If you don't believe in love, how can you hope to marry for it?'

Their drinks and food arrived. Emma reached for her iced coffee with a trembling hand. She didn't know what to say to him now. What could she possibly say that wouldn't give her stupid, romantic heart away?

'Darling,' Patrick drawled insincerely, 'I'm going to start thinking you've fallen in love with me if you don't answer right away.'

She gave a light, sophisticated, blasé laugh. 'Don't be so silly!' she mocked, trembling like a leaf, her heart banging so loudly she was afraid he would hear it.

'Well, then.' He sipped his iced coffee. 'Let's just say, The hell with it all, and get married. That way, we can both live our own lives without getting caught up in emotional rubbish.'

Her heart contracted as though stabbed. 'Well...I suppose it's an idea.' How could she say anything else? If she went on about marrying for love, he would suspect her of having fallen—very recently—in love with someone. Even the most stupid man in the world would put two and two together and come up with Patrick Kinsella, and Patrick Kinsella was hardly stupid. 'And we can always change our minds after a few weeks, decide against going through with it.'

'Then that's settled,' he drawled, studying her with that cold, cynical smile. 'For the moment, we're going through with the marriage. So we'd better discuss the logistics.'

'Yes, let's.' She was fighting so hard to remain cynical, not to show her love, the depths of her pain, her agony...

'I suggest we get it over with quickly. If we drag it out, we'll only make it worse.'

'I agree.' She couldn't believe this was happening. The words were coming out of her cool, sophisticated mouth but she seemed to have no control over them, as though pride had grown so strong, so difficult to maintain, that she could only keep it up as a barrier by ceasing to exist emotionally, and behaving like a robot.

She wanted to break down and cry. She wanted to tell him she was in love with him, that he had made her fall in love with him, that he had destroyed her life, her capacity to love anyone else, and that if she married him in these circumstances it would kill her heart forever.

But she didn't do any of that.

She just smiled coolly, her face serenely cynical, and agreed with everything he said.

'I don't think we should stay on the ship, though,' Patrick was drawling in his cynical way. 'We'd never be able to keep up the act of being a normal, loving couple about to get married.'

'Definitely not, darling!' she drawled with a sophisticated laugh.

'I therefore suggest,' he went on coolly, 'that we leave the ship and disappear somewhere together in a pretend elopement.'

'Excellent idea, darling! But where would we go?'

'Ireland?' he suggested coolly, and her heart stopped beating.

The rush of cool water from the fountains was all around them, as was birdsong from the open roof above the palms, and as Emma stared at Patrick she knew that silly, romantic heart of hers was trying desperately to stand up again, to resurrect itself from its long-forgotten grave.

Of course, he couldn't mean it. He couldn't be thinking of taking her to Ireland, because if he was it must mean he was serious about marrying her, and wanted to propose to her properly, in the one country where the deepest, most romantic part of herself had been consigned to the secrecy of forbidden blood since her birth.

'What do you think?' He wasn't looking at her, examining his glass of iced coffee instead. 'It might be worth a try.'

It took her several seconds to find her voice. She felt so deeply in love, and so terrified of her feelings, that it took all her self-control to remain cool and unemotional.

'I suppose it might be worth a try.'

He tensed, but smiled, and said, 'We'll fly to Ireland tomorrow, then. I can have a plane organised to meet us at Madeira in the morning and take us straight there.'

'Yes,' she drawled, 'why not?'

He looked at her then, and her heart spun somersaults at the dark communion in those blue eyes of his, because she knew, she just knew that he loved her, that he wanted to marry her, that dreams did come true...

Terror rose up to drown her romanticism, and she jerked her gaze away, struggling to be sensible, to be realistic and, above all, to avoid making a colossal fool of herself by leaping to silly, romantic conclusions that might not necessarily be the right ones.

'After all,' she said in a highly strung voice, 'it will certainly do us both good to get away from the ship. Everything's been so intense since this cruise began. Ireland will probably bring us back down to earth with a healthy bump and make us realise there's nothing very much between us at all. Good heavens——' she laughed with blasé mockery '—we'll probably jettison this stupid idea of marriage altogether, and go our own separate ways!'

'As you've never been to Ireland,' he said thickly, his mouth tightening to a white line, 'I hardly think you have the authority to say that.' He pushed his glass angrily away, got to his feet. 'Come on. Let's do some sightseeing. Suddenly I'm not hungry any more.'

She got shakily to her feet, staring at him, thinking, Is he hurt? then telling herself he couldn't be, couldn't possibly be, and she was so afraid of being wrong that she just said nothing, and walked out of the hotel in his dynamic wake.

They drove across the city in brooding silence. Emma wondered if she should say something to counteract what she had so insensitively said earlier, but how could she do that without making it clear that she really was in love with him, and trying to hide it?

The horror she felt at the thought of him either finding out or realising that she loved him was quite unbelievable, and certainly kept her silent. She was only too well aware of her capacity for blurting out truths—particularly to Patrick—and the last thing she wanted to do was blurt that little secret out.

He stopped the car at the tomb of Mohammed.

Rows of cool white pillars stood in a gleaming courtyard beside the vast, gilt-edged temple building. Armed guards watched tourists walk around taking photographs. The sun was very hot.

In tense silence, Patrick and Emma walked into the temple and stood in the mosaiced, gilt-edged stone room, staring down at the beautiful marble coffin.

'We all have to bow,' drawled Patrick, 'in order to see his coffin.'

'Maybe you should be buried like this,' Emma quipped, giving him a haughty look. 'I'm sure the idea appeals.'

'I don't see that death is an appropriate subject for that kind of humour.'

Her eyes flashed as she drawled, 'I agree. But you know, the funniest thing is that I often think of you in connection with death. I wonder if that means anything?'

'Who knows?' he drawled thickly, eyes very dark. 'Maybe we were lovers in a past life.'

'We're certainly not lovers in this life. I got away with it last night, I'm sure I can do it again—Ireland or no Ireland, ring or no ring, marriage or no marriage!' She watched him with a cool smile, while inside her emotions flew like the Furies. 'And, speaking of last night, I seem to remember you making a promise to tell me all about your late wife.'

He looked at her, his face hardening, and as his lashes flickered on those tough, angular cheekbones he said, 'Let's go outside.'

Emma's mouth tightened, but she allowed him to take her arm and lead her out into the hot sunlight, across the white terrace to the green-gold railings which enclosed the sacred ruined temple area.

He leant on the railings beside her, very tall and very silent. She was certain that he would tell her little or nothing about his late wife, and she hated him for that, because he knew so much about her, and besides, he had promised. But what was one broken promise in a long line of lies and clever con-man playboy behaviour?

Swallowing on a lump in her throat, she looked up at his tanned face and tried to keep her own expression sophisticatedly cool.

'My wife...' murmured Patrick, unsmiling, and glanced down to see her surprised expression. 'Well, her name was Annabel, and she was everything my family wanted me to marry. Diplomat's daughter, first-class education, a lady in everything she did and said.'

'Sounds perfect.' Emma laughed lightly, feeling jealous.

'Well, that was the point,' he drawled. 'My parents were very hot on perfection and I bent over backwards to give it to them. Only trouble was, I built a big brick-walled prison around myself trying to *be* perfect, and Annabel was a part of that.'

His eyes were starry-night blue, and Emma felt as though she was looking into a mirror, which was scary, much too scary, so she looked away from his reflective eyes and struggled not to feel love cascading through her heart like sunlight.

'We married young,' he went on, 'and for years every-thing remained statically perfect. I was the perfect, faithful, hard-working husband. She was the perfect wife.'

'Did you have children?'

'No, but we tried to, endlessly. Annabel couldn't con-ceive. I went to the doctors to find out if the problem was with me, but it wasn't, and for a while we soldiered on with our perfect marriage, trying to pretend it didn't matter.'

'You wanted children?' she asked huskily.

'And that's when it all began to fall apart.' He leant on the railings, staring out at the white columns of the temple. 'You see, I found a pack of contraceptive pills hidden in the glove compartment of Annabel's Mercedes 200 SL.'

Emma caught her breath, staring in disbelief.

'She'd been taking them throughout our marriage and lying to me about it, because she knew how much I wanted children. I confronted her with them, we had a row to end all rows, and two weeks later I discovered something else.'

Emma held her breath now, waiting.

He turned to look at her, his face hard. 'She'd been having an affair with my best friend———'

'Oh, my God...'

'For three years.'

'Oh, no...' She couldn't help her sympathy, her understanding, her fellow-feeling at the horror he must have gone through.

'I drove round in a fury to see him,' Patrick drawled, 'and beat the living daylights out of him. Annabel tried to get there before me, went too fast, and drove her beautiful red Mercedes 200 SL straight into a large tree.'

Emma felt such deep horror and such powerful love that she couldn't speak, just stood there staring in breathless silence.

'As you can imagine,' he drawled sardonically, 'I did not invite my best friend to the funeral.'

'She died instantly?'

'On impact.'

Emma swallowed, staring into his face, feeling waves of love but afraid to show it in case she was imagining it, imagining that they had more in common than she had ever suspected.

'After that,' he went on coolly, 'I stopped believing in perfect love and marriage. In fact, I tore my perfect life into tiny shreds and went on a rampage, indulging every bad bit of blood I had. That's how I got the reputation you hate so much.'

Her lashes flickered as she studied him, love shining in her eyes. 'A reputation you clearly earned.'

'Do you blame me?' He swung to look at her, his face harsh.

Slowly, she shook her head, saying softly, 'No...'

There was a brief silence as they studied each other, and the dark communion in their eyes was so powerful that Emma felt moved with the depth of feeling between them.

'So——' Patrick looked away, glanced at the Rolex on his dark-haired wrist '—enough of memory lane. Time's moving on and we have to get back to the ship.'

Shaken, Emma walked with him back to the car, her legs as wobbly as her determination to hate him, to stop him getting the better of her.

As she slid into the front seat, she looked up into his tough face and almost shivered at the uncanny resemblance between their two souls. If fate had had them hand-knitted for each other, they could not have been more perfectly matched.

Patrick got in beside her, started the car, very cool, and they drove away into the mainstream of traffic in silence before shooting out of the city and into the endless, achingly beautiful desert.

I'm so much in love with him, she thought as she stared at the sands, seeing buzzards circling the corpse of some long-dead animal.

The understanding of his past was so very important to her that she felt as if one of the final pieces of a vastly complicated jigsaw puzzle had fallen into place. The very final piece was whether or not he loved her, and she suddenly felt desperate to know, desperate to have that final piece in place, so desperate that her whole life, everything she was, everything she ever had been—and everything she could be—seemed suddenly to depend on it.

She studied the desert and asked coolly, 'I can see why you didn't tell me about your wife last night. It was hardly the time or place. But Patrick...why didn't you tell me before?'

He was silent for a moment, then said coolly, 'Oh, I just never got around to it, that's all.'

'Even while,' she drawled lightly, 'you were gathering very similar information about me—and my past?'

'Well, of course,' he drawled, a cynical smile on his tough mouth.

Her heart skipped beats. He was being extremely cool, and that was precisely what she was being.

Was it possible that the extent of their mirrored souls extended far beyond similar pasts, and into similar reactions? If so, that meant only one thing—Patrick was as deeply in love with her as she was with him, and his cynicism was just a shield with which to mask it.

Hope sprang like wildfire in her heart, yet still she was frightened, still she couldn't bring herself to believe that love did exist, that it was real, and that she would find happiness with a man as wonderful, sensitive, intelligent, dynamic and sexy as Patrick Kinsella.

'Where will we stay in Ireland?' she asked coolly, not looking at him. 'You said you had a house there...'

'Yes, it's about two hours' drive from Dublin airport.' His voice was the epitome of a rich, international playboy's. 'I have other homes—in New York, London and Rome. But I'd prefer to go to Ireland.'

'Any good reason why?' she asked lightly, heart banging like mad.

'Not really,' he drawled with a lazy smile, 'but it'll be the perfect antidote to all this hot weather and tourism.'

Her lashes flickered. Romanticism was blazing in her eyes, her heart, her soul. He loves me, he loves me not, he loves me, he loves me not...

Oh, God, she was so scared, and so excited.

They drove on in silence, and Emma did not dare speak again, deeply aware of him beside her, of the power of his body, the strength of his character, the depth of his soul.

So he was a very bad boy, she thought with flutters of excitement, when he smashed his way out of his perfect world. No wonder he was so incredibly good at touching me last night in bed. No wonder he was such an exciting, wicked, experienced lover...

If she went to Ireland with him tomorrow as planned, she realised, he would undoubtedly expect her to make love with him.

She flicked her hot, emotional gaze to the long, powerful hands on the steering-wheel, and remembered how it had felt when those clever fingers had stroked her towards ecstasy last night.

Oh, God, she thought, yum, yum.

Yes, please.

Running a hand through her dark hair, she struggled for logic before feeling and sensation drove all common sense from her mind. He may not love you at all, Emma! she told herself fiercely. He may just be what he says he is—a cynical swine marrying you for expediency's sake.

The car slowed at the docks of Casablanca.

She sat listening to the engine purr as Patrick handed their documents to the Moroccan official, spoke briefly in French with him, then drove on to the hot, dirty dock.

He stopped the car, looked up at the great, glittering, multimillion-pound yacht, and gave a cynical smile.

'Everyone will be expecting us to be ecstatically in love,' he drawled. 'We'd better make it look convincing—touch each other a lot, kiss each other. Think you can do that for me?'

Her heart hammered with excitement, but she laughed and replied, 'Piece of cake, darling!'

'Then come here.' He reached for her with strong hands. 'I want that sexy little mouth of yours to look thoroughly kissed by the time we walk on board.'

His mouth opened hers commandingly and she couldn't fight it, couldn't stop the emotion welling up in her, kissing him back so fiercely that he groaned and fell on her in the front seat, lying suddenly on top of her, his powerful body already hard with pulsing excitement.

Their mouths ate each other hungrily. His hands moved over her breasts and she did not stop him, moaning with open pleasure against his lips, his tongue, his breath.

'Wow...!' he said thickly against her mouth, and his skin was so hot, it almost burned to touch it as he stared at her with eyes like blue fire. 'I can't wait to get you to Ireland.'

Emma's eyes were burning just as much as her bruised mouth murmured, 'I don't know that I'm going to let you seduce me tomorrow, Patrick. Don't count on it, will you?'

'Not in a million,' he drawled thickly, smiling like a true cynic, and kissed her again, deeply, his body pressing against hers with fierce passion.

Her response was so fervent that they both knew it was a hundred per cent certain that, had they been in a bed, he would very probably have made full love to her and elicited cries of intolerable pleasure from her.

To her surprise, he suddenly released her with a shove, his face flushed and his breathing ragged. 'That's enough. Come on. Let's get this show on the road.'

Emma blinked as he got out of the car. Her heart was banging like crazy. She was so aroused she could scarcely think, even the simplest movements difficult as she fumbled for the door-handle, shaking like a leaf, wanting him so much that she could barely stand.

Is he really my soulmate? she wondered in desperate emotional confusion. Am I imagining all of this? Is this really what being wildly in love feels like?

He stood waiting for her, tall, desirable and coolly dignified. Emma smiled, watching him through her lashes as she moved towards him, and he smiled back like a lazy tiger, linking his strong hand with hers in a gesture that made her believe that he loved her.

Yet still she was afraid...

Together, they walked to the yacht.

'Hey, look!' shouted Charles from the deck. 'It's the bride and groom!'

'I know,' Toby said wryly. 'They've just been eating each other in the front of the car. Some guys have all the luck.'

Patrick smiled and shot a wicked, glinting look at Emma through his black lashes, making her heart skip beats as she met that gaze, loving him, wanting him, fearing all her dizzy emotions...

'They look very het up to me,' Natasha said nastily. 'Maybe they've had a row and changed their minds.'

'We're perfectly happy, thank you,' Patrick clipped out coldly as he strode up the gangplank with Emma. 'We just have a lot to do before we leave tomorrow.'

'Leave tomorrow!' Liz stared at her brother. 'What are you talking about?'

Patrick released Emma's hand and strode to the drinks table, pouring himself a large whisky. 'We've decided we need some privacy, so we're flying off to be alone together. Sorry and all that. Hope you can manage without us.'

They all stared in horror.

Patrick looked at Emma with a lazy smile. 'Drink?'

'Thanks, I'd love one, darling!' She laughed breath-
lessly and walked towards him, putting her arms around
his powerful chest, playing the happy fiancée for all it
was worth while deep inside she wanted to bow her head,
give up her pride, and tell him she loved him desperately, every inch of him, every point on the map of his
life, and every moment of wickedness in the name of
freedom.

Patrick laughed too, and bent his head to kiss her
mouth. 'I want to get absolutely plastered tonight—must
be wedding nerves! How about you?'

'Plastered out of my head, darling!' The huskiness in
her voice was so deep, she knew it told him of her love.

For a second he stared at her. Then suddenly he put
down the bottle with a crash, pulled her clumsily into
his arms and kissed her with an intensity that made her
breathless, her hands pushing into his dark hair, her eyes
closed and her body pressing tightly against his.

'Well!' breathed Natasha behind them, speechless for
once.

Patrick broke off the kiss, and raised his head, face
flushed, eyes glittering. Emma swayed in his arms, her
legs buckling as she stumbled away, trying not to look
emotional while breathing hoarsely.

God, she thought, I can't believe I can love someone
this much and keep it hidden.

'Very passionate,' said Charles, watching them with
a smile. 'I wonder if we ought to leave you two to cel-
ebrate alone?'

'Yes, we're only going to be in the way,' Liz agreed.

'No,' Patrick said thickly, shaking his dark head.
'There are a number of things I have to do before we
leave tomorrow. I'll just skip dinner and go to my study,
if you don't mind. Sorry, darling——' he looked down

at Emma with blazing, passionate eyes '—but I've got to organise that jet, among other things. You stay with the others. I'll see you in the morning.'

Emma murmured something incomprehensible.

'I'll come and wake you up,' he drawled softly, and bent his dark head to kiss her mouth before winking coolly, and striding away without another word.

She watched him go, her heart pounding. What did that mean? Had he put on that sudden passionate, loving display for the benefit of everyone else?

Or had he taken the opportunity to show his love, for the first time, just as she had done?

CHAPTER TEN

IT WAS a sleepless night for Emma, one in which she felt sick, her palms sweated, her body drummed with insatiable desire, and she generally spent hours pacing her cabin, running frantic hands through her hair, thinking of tomorrow, wondering if he loved her, piecing together everything he had ever said to her, everything, down to the last sentence, the last word, the last look, touch, smile...

He must love me, she finally thought with blinding clarity, then five seconds later, No, he doesn't!

Veering between heaven and hell all night, she was kept company by the ship's engines, the lapping of the midnight-blue sea outside her window, and the gentle rocking of the yacht as they sailed across the coast of Africa towards Madeira.

She fell asleep as dawn broke, and was awakened at twelve by a loud, peremptory knocking on the door. Jerking upright, she stared around in confusion, then heard the knuckles rapping on the door again and jumped up to run to it.

Patrick towered over her in the doorway. He looked tense and ill, his eyes burning with an almost unnatural excitement, and she wondered if he felt as sick to his stomach with tension as she did.

'We dock in fifteen minutes,' he said thickly. 'Are you ready to leave immediately?'

'Yes, I packed last night.' Her voice shook, her heart pounded, and she felt acutely ready for lovemaking as his eyes moved over her body in the strappy white satin nightdress.

'Good.' He turned away as though afraid to look at her in case he leapt on her. 'I'll see you on deck, then.'

Emma shut the door, breathing erratically, then ran to the bathroom and took a shower, blow-drying her long dark hair minutes later, the whoosh of the hairdrier comfortingly familiar in a dislocated world.

Dressing carefully in her chosen outfit, she hoped she looked suitable for both Madeira and Ireland. The black skirt was loose, elegant, falling to just above her ankles in soft, fluid lines, a slit running to her knees to make it easier to walk quickly. She wore a soft green blouse with it and carried a long black jacket. Her shoes were flat, elegant, black.

A steward came to help her with her cases.

Up on deck, gulls were flying around the yacht while Madeira towered before them like a tropical dream, covered in lush plants, trees, shrubs, flowers, all growing in wild profusion in its fertile soil, while down along the waterfront pink Portuguese palaces gleamed under the hot sun.

Emma felt strangely unreal, standing there saying goodbye to everyone. The breeze lifted her dark hair softly, and she knew she was alive, that nothing had changed in the outer world, but inside, inside...

How could the world be so different when one was in love? Perhaps that was why people spent so long searching for it, because life only made sense once love finally came. It was the Holy Grail—or the only antidote to death.

'I'll speak to you some time soon,' Liz whispered in her ear as she kissed her, 'and I'll miss you.'

Emma smiled, kissed her back. 'I'll miss you too.' But as she said it she knew it was untrue. Nothing existed for her now. Nothing but Patrick, and as she lifted her head to look at him she knew she had already stepped into another world, entered a new dimension with him, and that they were about to be sealed off together forever inside it.

She had ceased trying to find explanations for the inexplicable, and that, she thought suddenly, had been a very necessary thing to do because, as she had always known and feared, love was one of the major areas of life that was beyond one's control.

A bright yellow taxi with a blue strip down the side waited for them with its engine purring. The stewards were loading their cases into the trunk.

Patrick put a hand under her elbow. 'Time we went.'

She nodded, walked with him to the gangplank, took one last look at them all over her shoulder, smiling, and said, 'Goodbye...'

They all waved and called goodbye, then Patrick led her down the gangplank to the taxi, put her in the rear seat, slid in beside her, and told the driver to take them to Funchal airport.

'How do you feel?' he asked coolly.

'I...' She struggled to sound cool too. 'I must admit, I feel rather weird! Going off to Ireland to marry a strange man.'

'I don't mind being described as strange——' his eyes glittered with answering amusement '—but would you rather I was ordinary?'

'Oh, God, no!' She laughed with sophisticated humour. 'Ordinary men are so perfect, and I've had enough of perfection to last me a lifetime.'

'Me too,' he murmured, smiling cynically, his eyes very blue.

'Besides, ordinary men always detest me, anyway. Clearly it's my destiny to be just as strange as you are. Perhaps we're well-matched.'

'Locking together,' he said softly, 'in mirrored imperfection.'

Their eyes met and emotion blazed between them so fiercely that Emma shook with it, and she thought, He must love me. He must. That's what every moment of this has been about, why he's chased me so hard, and why our lives seem to mirror each other in that wonderful imperfection.

Then she looked away from him, her pulses throbbing so violently that she had to fight to stay serene, cool, sophisticated.

The drive to the airport was exquisitely tense.

His private jet was waiting on the black tarmac. It was white and sleek and very powerful-looking. Emma looked at it with amused detachment. How very odd that she should fall in love with a rich man without even noticing that he was rich. How many times had she heard friends say that they wanted to fall in love with a multi-millionaire? And how could she possibly see Patrick as one, when she saw him only as a man—and the man she loved at that?

They boarded the jet after clearing Customs. In the dove-grey luxurious interior, a set of smiling stewardesses began attending to their every need, making Emma study them with cool jealousy when they fawned over Patrick. He was amused by her cool jealousy, of course, and smiled lazily at her as they sat together in luxurious seats as big as armchairs. The stewardesses disappeared, leaving them alone together, which was the first thing they'd done to please Emma.

The engines whined softly, then they began to taxi slowly towards the runway.

'Will it take us straight to Ireland?' she asked him.

'I had to move a few mountains to get the flight path at such short notice,' he murmured with a cool smile, 'but I managed it in the end.'

Emma laughed drily. 'Must be nice to be rich and powerful!'

His smile tensed. 'You're not going to start talking about money again, are you?'

'No,' she said simply, struggling to be honest instead of cynical. 'It doesn't bother me that much any more. I hated it when I thought it was all you were interested in, just as I hated you when I thought you were only interested in sex.'

'And you no longer think that, do you?'

'No...' Her voice was terribly husky with emotion as she looked at him. 'As for your money—well, it's just something that's part of the real world for you.'

'Ah, yes... the real world.' He watched her with dark eyes.

'But we don't live there, do we?' she said huskily, her heart banging like mad as she took a chance, a terrible risk, looking straight into his eyes, needing confirmation that he really *was* feeling what she was feeling.

'In the real world?' he asked deeply, his eyes holding hers and matching them. 'No, we live somewhere quite different where money can't touch us.'

Her eyes blazed with love. 'Do you mean that, Patrick?'

His hand closed over hers, she saw the emotion in his eyes, and then he leaned over to kiss her mouth, kissing her deeply, one hand on her face, the other clutching her fingers tight, his mouth passionate and tender.

'Ready for take-off, Mr Kinsella,' the captain said over the Tannoy. 'Cabin staff to your seats, please.'

Patrick broke off the kiss with reluctance, leaning back in his seat, but he did not relinquish her hand, and as their fingers locked in a tight, silent admission of love Emma thought, Please let this be true, please let him really, really love me . . .

The engines built rapidly, the plane jolted forward, and they roared along the notorious Funchal runway at terrifying speed, the ground flashing faster and faster beneath them as they approached that jut of tarmac straight above the sea, then lifted, miraculously, into the air in a steady upward ascent to the cloudless blue sky.

The flight took several hours.

They talked all the time, their hands linked and their eyes meeting in dark admission of love. He told her about his perfect life, and she smiled with pride at the list of accolades he had won through school, university, and on into his business life, climbing higher, higher, up into the stratosphere with achievement, money and power until he'd realised how worthless and shallow it all was without honesty, truth and love.

The stewardesses brought them coffee, a light snack. The jet flew on across Europe. And still they talked, their heads together, hands linked, voices lowered with intimate trust. Emma told him about her childhood, and about the way she had played the perfect daughter, first in school, then in life, pursuing stupid, shallow achievements that she detested, just in order to win her father's approval.

'He used his money to buy me too,' she was saying as they began their descent into Dublin airport. 'In fact, it's a strange coincidence, but the car he bought me for my twenty-first birthday was the same as the car you bought Annabel.'

'Hardly a strange coincidence, darling,' he said with a wry smile. 'Not among all the other strange coincidences between us.'

She looked into his eyes, her heart spinning with love, and thought, I wonder if we'll ever both be able to admit how we feel?

As they flew into Dublin, it was raining. Emma smiled wryly as she watched the raindrops blowing across the plane windows, saw the grey skies, the wild green land stretching out just as she had always imagined it, and a few minutes later they were landing with a smooth touch on the wet tarmac.

'I always thought I'd think of my mother when I first arrived in Ireland,' Emma commented quietly. 'But I'm not thinking of her at all. I'm thinking of something quite different . . .'

'What?' he asked at her side.

She smiled and said, 'I always thought it would be magical, you see, and romantic. But it's not. It's just ordinary and natural, and all I can think of is that I've reached the end of a very long journey. As though I've come home to something inside myself.'

He raised her hand to his mouth, kissed the slender fingers, and then the door was opened, the steps were brought, and minutes later they were disembarking together.

A helicopter was waiting in another part of the airport, and they were driven there after clearing Customs. The cool Irish wind whipped Emma's hair around her rain-wet face as she climbed into the sleek black craft. Money and power were stamped over everything Patrick Kinsella touched, that much was obvious. But she was so completely inside their secret, private, inner world that she took the symbols of his money and power for the strange little symbols that they were. They had nothing to do with their love. Yes, they were part of his life. Yes, they were wonderful to have around. But no, they did not constitute one-tenth of her love for him, and no, they would not save either of them from death.

'I might have known it would be raining and windy,' Patrick drawled as he closed the helicopter door, relaxed in the seat beside her, and watched the pilot start flicking switches in preparation for take-off.

'Oh, I'm glad it is,' she said with a smile. 'It makes everything seem much more real than all that sunshine on the yacht.'

He laughed. 'It does get rather tedious, doesn't it?'

The helicopter lifted off. Emma's hand was enfolded by Patrick's. They were moving deeper and deeper into their private world. Soon it would be sealed forever, but they were content to wait for the door to slam, now that they were both finally confident that it would.

'Did you have a good trip, sir?' the pilot asked above the noise of the whirring blades, and both Emma and Patrick just looked at him dispassionately because he did not belong to their private world, just as nobody else did.

'Yes,' Patrick said, well-mannered as always, a cool smile on his mouth, 'very good. How was your summer, Sean?'

'Oh, marvellous, sir!' the pilot called back cheerfully, and the craft steered across the storm-tossed skies.

Soon the helicopter was descending over a large grey-white manor house standing in secluded land, rich green grass as far as the eye could see, a sprinkling of trees surrounding it at the borders, horses running wild and free in the rain.

Two men and a woman stood on the top lawn as the helicopter came in to land on the flattest area of the grass. The blades sent trees bending back and forth, leaves scurrying wetly from their cowed branches, and a second later they bounced gently to a standstill.

Climbing out, Patrick turned, extended a strong hand to her, and Emma stepped out, her hair whipping wildly in the fierce wind generated by the blades above. He stared down at her in silence, and she smiled at him, unaware of her beauty, the blazing green of her eyes, the look of love touching every part of her face as she stood there, her hand in his.

'Welcome home, Mr Kinsella!' a man's smooth Irish voice shouted above the noise of the helicopter. 'We have your rooms made ready, and the housekeeper wishes to discuss dinner with——'

'We won't be eating,' Patrick said. 'Thank you all the same, but just go about your business as usual. Have our cases stored in the hall for the moment and don't disturb us. We'll go straight up to our rooms.'

Emma didn't contradict him, smiling as she walked with him across the grass to the manor house, the helicopter noise dying down as they walked up a set of grey-white steps to a pair of double doors flung wide in welcome.

Their footsteps rang out across the marble hallway. They walked to the stairs, which were wide and sweeping, covered in dull red carpet, lined by paintings, illuminated by a big crystal chandelier that tinkled softly in the breeze from the open doors. He led her up, along a wide high-ceilinged corridor, then stopped at a big oak door and looked down at her, his eyes veiled.

'This is the master bedroom,' he said.

'And this is the master,' she murmured, smiling at him through her lashes.

He laughed, and pushed open the door. She walked inside, her step light and quick, and all she saw was the big four-poster double bed hung with dark curtains.

The door closed. She turned, and as her eyes met his she was gripped by the most primitive emotions, love clamouring to be expressed, her eyes blazing fierce green with it.

Patrick walked towards her, his hands in his pockets, and stopped in front of her, towering over her.

There was a brief, tense silence.

'Of course,' he said deeply, 'you know I'm in love with you?'

Her heart somersaulted and her eyes closed. 'Darling, yes... yes! And I'm in love with you.'

'And you know——' his voice was even deeper '—that that ring on your finger is no pretence?'

Her eyes opened, dark with love.

'I'm asking you to marry me, Emma.'

'Oh, Patrick...'

'Tell me the answer is yes.'

'What else could it possibly be?'

He put his arms around her tenderly, kissed her neck, whispered, 'When did you know you loved me?'

'From the start,' she whispered back, clinging to him, eyes closed, astonished at the speed of this declaration, and the deeply natural feel of it, the way they had simply stopped pretending as soon as they'd left the ship, as soon as they'd each found the confidence to grope for the other's hand, and link their love in truth, not fear and lies. 'Patrick, I fought it because I was afraid. I've never been in love before. Never.'

'No, neither have I,' he said deeply, raising his head to look at her with those wonderfully blue, deeply sensitive eyes. 'And now that I am, I can see precisely why.'

'Because you fall in love,' she said softly, understanding completely, 'when you least expect it.'

'When you stop looking for it.' His smile was touchingly sweet on such a powerful man. 'I think the truth is that we both spent most of our lives wanting to be in love. I can see clearly now that I did. OK, I hated the pretence when I realised that was what it was, but it took betrayal to make me see it. Up until then I was floating about in a romantic daydream. When the betrayal came, it hit so hard that I never recovered ... until I met you.'

'No,' she said huskily, stroking his strong neck, 'I think you'd recovered before you met me. Otherwise, how could you have fallen in love so rapidly?'

He laughed. 'Rapidly! My God, I fell in seconds! I can remember standing there on that wretched deck with you, telling you how isolated I sometimes felt, hearing that you felt the same, understanding why, and then— wham! I was dropping in a lift, seventy-five floors in two seconds!'

'Horrifying, wasn't it?'

'You did feel the same, didn't you?' He raised his head, kissed her mouth tenderly. 'I was sure you did, but I was so terrified that I was imagining it, and every shred of logic I had was fighting like mad.'

'I fought just as hard, darling.'

'I thought it was because I didn't want to fall in love. But that wasn't the case at all. It was the reverse. I wanted to believe in love so badly that I was terrified by my sudden capacity for romance.'

'So was I, Patrick.' Her eyes were filled with love. 'Right up until we left the ship I was still fighting like mad, just in case I was going to make a fool of myself, just in case I was letting romanticism take hold, just in case it was all a foolish dream.'

'You were doing that all along, darling, and I knew it. At least I had my reputation as a playboy to shield my true feelings from you, but you didn't have anything.'

'That's why you were able to keep banging on my door, pretending you were only interested in seduction.'

'I didn't actually do that, darling,' he said, arching dark brows. 'I really did keep telling you there was more between us than that.'

'But I was too afraid to believe you.'

He smiled. 'And when did you start believing I was telling the truth?'

She blushed delicate pink, said softly, 'Not until you released me. That was when I really crumbled, let my defences go, let myself believe in love again. You could so easily have taken me, and I wouldn't have been able to stop you. Not at that point.'

'It was wonderful waking up with you the next morning.' He bent his strong head to kiss her mouth. 'I felt completely unafraid of showing affection, real affection. I could have stayed cuddling in that bed with you forever.'

'Yes, I felt wonderful too. Cleansed and natural and completely whole. As though none of the bad stuff ever happened, or, if it did, it was only to prepare me for you.'

'We can begin living now, darling,' he said softly, stroking her hair with strong, tender fingers. 'No more getting side-tracked by rage, no more lies or pretence or refusal to believe in the good in people. We can live in a realistic paradise together, make love, be loved, have children—and even see bluebirds if we want to, without ever having to pay the price.'

She laughed softly. 'I've been seeing bluebirds since I met you!'

'Horrors, darling!' he drawled, eyes glinting. 'Simply *must* be the champagne!'

'Patrick...' She hesitated, her heart skipping. 'Did you just mention children?'

'Yes...'

'Then this is really happening?' Tears filled her eyes. 'We really are in love, we're going to get married, stay together, and have lots of children? Just like in Liz's novels?'

He kissed her tenderly, whispering, 'Just like it, darling. I mean every word I say. Please never doubt my sincerity.'

'Oh, I never thought this would happen to me—never!' She fought the vast onslaught of emotion blazing through her, her hands shaking on his broad shoulders as she kissed him back passionately. 'Darling, I can't believe how wonderful life suddenly seems! Just think of the life we can share, the fun we can have, the conversations, the lovemaking——'

'Oh, yes,' he said deeply, 'just think...'

Her eyes met his. 'I—I often feel with you that it goes beyond lovemaking. It's not like seduction or sex or lust, is it? It's altogether more human than that, more necessary, all wrapped up with life and death, somehow.'

'The urge to mate,' he said thickly, staring into her eyes.

'Like animals,' she whispered.

'Lion... and lioness.'

'Patrick, I've thought that so often! Have you thought it too?'

'Ever since that first night,' he said roughly, 'when I looked at you and wanted you so violently I would have torn your clothes off and taken you on the spot if I hadn't been a civilised man in a civilised world.'

The impression of an electric current running between them was suddenly so strong that they were both immobile, caught in its grip, staring at one another.

Emma shuddered passionately. 'I love you. Make love to me.'

He lowered his dark head with serious intent, his mouth met hers, and as they kissed the passion flared between them like wildfire, making each moan with sudden appalled desire.

A second later they were falling back on to the bed, their mouths locked together while their hands began tearing at each other's clothes.

His jacket fell to the floor. His eyes were tightly shut, his breathing fierce, and Emma moaned under his kiss, her mouth hot. All she could think of was total physical union, and for the first time in her life she wanted it, really wanted it, wanted it so much that she would die, if necessary, to get it.

Her mind kept throwing up violent, searing images of his body entering hers, as though nothing would ever be real for her unless she could feel that rigid flesh penetrating her body, filling her, making her female, yet not female—uniting their souls as their bodies joined to wipe out the sexes and make them one.

She tore at his shirt in desperate haste. She could imagine how it was to be a man, suddenly, as though his flesh were hers, as though they were more than blending in their physical union, as though they were almost capable of changing places at explosion point.

His hands were shaking as they pushed her jacket off too, then started fumbling with the buttons of her green blouse. She helped him, gasping his name hoarsely as together they tore the green silk away, threw it aside, freed her breasts from the confines of an irrelevant, utterly pointless bra.

They wasted little time on preliminaries.

They were too excited.

Kissing hungrily, they were obsessed by one drive and one drive only: the urge to mate.

She was as desperate as he, her hands moving over the belt of his trousers, unbuckling it as she moaned against his hot mouth, moving her body provocatively, inflaming him to hoarse cries of desire.

He was naked suddenly.

So was she.

Their skins were so hot they were covered in sweat, both shaking with excitement, rolling together in slow undulations like a two-headed creature.

His fingers slid to the hot, fierce wetness between her legs. She moaned deliriously, opened to him, let her body slide against his fingers with blatant desire. As he whispered incoherently against her bare, hot throat, she let her hands move down to touch the hot, hard evidence of his sex, and moaned again as she heard him give a hoarse cry of agony, pushing against her hands, pushing, pushing, pushing...

He slid between her thighs and entered her.

'Oh, God...!' Her voice was guttural, her neck rigid with sexual tension, her hands clutched his lean hips and then she felt his manhood pulse and burn inside her, filling her, making her complete.

She felt the orgasm overpower her from behind her tortured mind, sending her into hot, wet spasms all over him, and she cried out into dark space with her eyes closed and her tongue protruding and everything spinning into the void.

Patrick was rigid, quivering inside her, grinding his teeth together in unrestrained excitement as he watched her hot, damp body fling itself into sweaty, uninhibited ecstasy.

When she was still, he dragged air into his lungs, tightened his mouth like an animal, then thrust himself deeper, deeper, faster, faster, until he went into spasms of electrifying intensity, his head thrown back, body

pumping life inside her womb, spurting inside her as
helplessly as though an artery had been severed, while
his voice cried out in harsh satisfaction.

He collapsed on her damp shoulder, shaking from
head to foot and gasping for breath. Emma lay shaking
beneath him, her arms around him, wondering if this
had all really happened, if what she thought had happened could possibly be true, and then smiled as tears
stung her eyes, because she knew that it was, and it was
only the last death-throes of her fear, her stupid cynicism,
that made her doubt him.

'So much for not believing in love!' Patrick said
huskily against her hot skin.

She laughed shakily, kissing his hot, wet throat. 'I
know. Isn't it absurd?'

'Completely.' He raised his head, blue eyes glittering
with love. 'But it was worth waiting a lifetime for.'

'Yes, a lifetime ...'

'They say there's only one true love in anyone's life,'
he murmured against her mouth. 'This is definitely it,
Emma. Complete mental, physical, spiritual and
emotional union. The big four. What more could anyone
ask for?'

'Nothing,' she said, her eyes filling with tears, 'absolutely nothing.'

He studied her with a smile. 'Where do you want to
live? I have so many homes, remember, and I do fly
around a lot on business. I'd love you to come with me
as often as possible, but if you prefer not to——'

'No, no, I definitely want to be with you as often as
I can.'

'What about your job with Liz? Do you want to keep
that up once we're married?'

She laughed softly, stroked his damp, dark hair. 'Well, you never know, darling. After what's happened to me, I might end up writing my own romantic novels instead! I'm certainly qualified now, and there's no doubt but that I believe in them!'

'Oh, God, how hilarious! Liz will never let us hear the end of it!' He grinned, kissing her mouth. 'Still, I guess I can put up with that. She did introduce us, after all. Credit where credit is due. And she always said I'd get my come-uppance one day, by falling heavily in love when I least expected it.'

'Yes, she said that the day I arrived, didn't she?'

'And I laughed at her,' he drawled wryly. 'Committing hubris like mad, darling. Serves me bloody well right. I was heavily in love within twenty-four hours.'

Emma kissed him lingeringly. 'Fate threw us together, not Liz. It was definitely fate. I was ready to fall in love, so were you—we just neither of us recognised it as that. And if I'd once seen you as anything other than detestable, I would never have been so honest with you, we would never have reached that point of mutual recognition—and we would never have fallen in love.'

He studied her with dark, dark eyes. 'Falling in love...so easy to say now, and so easy to think about. How did I ever hate the world so much that I annexed myself from love completely?'

'Because the world hurt you so badly, darling, just as it did me,' she said huskily, kissing his strong neck. 'And it took years for us both to set that pain down just long enough to be surprised by love.'

'And how easily it all came back to us both,' he murmured, smiling. 'We only met a few days ago, but I guess it's just something one never loses, no matter how bad it gets, no matter how many betrayals and set-backs and disillusionments there have been.'

'The ability to love,' she agreed softly, 'is always there, just waiting for a chance to express itself.'

His dark lashes flickered. 'What could be more natural?' he said deeply, and bent his head to kiss her.

Nothing, she thought as her eyes closed. Nothing could be more natural...

HARLEQUIN®

Don't miss these Harlequin favorites by some of our most distinguished authors!
And now, you can receive a discount by ordering two or more titles!

HT#25645	THREE GROOMS AND A WIFE by JoAnn Ross	$3.25 U.S. / $3.75 CAN.	☐
HT#25647	NOT THIS GUY by Glenda Sanders	$3.25 U.S. / $3.75 CAN.	☐
HP#11725	THE WRONG KIND OF WIFE by Roberta Leigh	$3.25 U.S. / $3.75 CAN.	☐
HP#11755	TIGER EYES by Robyn Donald	$3.25 U.S. / $3.75 CAN.	☐
HR#03416	A WIFE IN WAITING by Jessica Steele	$3.25 U.S. / $3.75 CAN.	☐
HR#03419	KIT AND THE COWBOY by Rebecca Winters	$3.25 U.S. / $3.75 CAN.	☐
HS#70622	KIM & THE COWBOY by Margot Dalton	$3.50 U.S. / $3.99 CAN.	☐
HS#70642	MONDAY'S CHILD by Janice Kaiser	$3.75 U.S. / $4.25 CAN.	☐
HI#22342	BABY VS. THE BAR by M.J. Rodgers	$3.50 U.S. / $3.99 CAN.	☐
HI#22382	SEE ME IN YOUR DREAMS by Patricia Rosemoor	$3.75 U.S. / $4.25 CAN.	☐
HAR#16538	KISSED BY THE SEA by Rebecca Flanders	$3.50 U.S. / $3.99 CAN.	☐
HAR#16603	MOMMY ON BOARD by Muriel Jensen	$3.50 U.S. / $3.99 CAN.	☐
HH#28885	DESERT ROGUE by Erine Yorke	$4.50 U.S. / $4.99 CAN.	☐
HH#28911	THE NORMAN'S HEART by Margaret Moore	$4.50 U.S. / $4.99 CAN.	☐

(limited quantities available on certain titles)

	AMOUNT	$
DEDUCT:	10% DISCOUNT FOR 2+ BOOKS	$
ADD:	POSTAGE & HANDLING	$
	($1.00 for one book, 50¢ for each additional)	
	APPLICABLE TAXES*	$_____
	TOTAL PAYABLE	$_____
	(check or money order—please do not send cash)	

To order, complete this form and send it, along with a check or money order for the total above, payable to Harlequin Books, to: **In the U.S.:** 3010 Walden Avenue, P.O. Box 9047, Buffalo, NY 14269-9047; **In Canada:** P.O. Box 613, Fort Erie, Ontario, L2A 5X3.

Name: _____

Address: _____ City: _____

State/Prov.: _____ Zip/Postal Code: _____

*New York residents remit applicable sales taxes.
 Canadian residents remit applicable GST and provincial taxes.

Look us up on-line at: http://www.romance.net

HBACK-JM4

HARLEQUIN PRESENTS®

The Marriage Maker
by
Robyn Donald

Can a picture from the past bring love to the present?

Coming next month:
the third and last story in
Robyn Donald's captivating new trilogy

#1877 THE FINAL PROPOSAL
Jan's Story

Available in April wherever
Harlequin books are sold.

HARLEQUIN ◆ PRESENTS®

"A prolonged stay in my harem will provide me
with a long-awaited opportunity to teach you
what being a woman is all about."

Will Bethany pay the price that Crown Prince Razul
is demanding—and become his wife?

Watch for
#1875 THE DESERT BRIDE
by
Lynne Graham

Available wherever Harlequin books are sold.

HARLEQUIN® Temptation

and

HARLEQUIN®

INTRIGUE®

Double Dare ya!

Identical twin authors Patricia Ryan and
Pamela Burford bring you a dynamic duo of
books that just happen to feature identical twins.

Meet Emma, the shy one, and her diva double,
Zara. Be prepared for twice the pleasure and
twice the excitement as they give two
unsuspecting men trouble times two!

In April, the scorching **Harlequin Temptation** novel
#631 **Twice the Spice** by Patricia Ryan

In May, the suspenseful **Harlequin Intrigue** novel
#420 **Twice Burned** by Pamela Burford

Pick up both—if you dare....

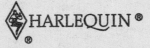

HARLEQUIN®

Look us up on-line at: http://www.romance.net   TWIN